AUTISM, ARE YOU F*&KING SERIOUS?

12 Honest Chapters About Parenting An Autistic Child

Written By Nick's Mom

Edited By Sarah Newton-John

ISBN-978-1-63625-194-3

Cover design by: Canva Pro Stock Images, Rendering done by Catherine Raleigh
Library of Congress Control Number: 2020922782
Printed in the United States of America

ISBN Summary

by Editor Sarah Newton-John

Nick's Mom knew there was something very different about her son. Here is the raw, honest and informative account of her journey through the diagnosis of his severe classic autism – the rather underwhelming world of medical support, some heartbreaking episodes, her avid learning about medications each day and ultimately the power of love that underpins her parenting of young Nicholas. This piece was written by someone who is in a position to speak through her experiences and save other parents from stress, confusion and frustration as they must adapt to raising an autistic child. This true story is not for the fainthearted or those seeking neat, easy messages. This writer is wise far beyond her years, and her extremely difficult circumstances are related with wit, laconic humour, absolute transparency and true grit. Her insights are relevant to readers whose lives are touched by this rather mysterious condition, and who will benefit from witnessing her ballsy, steadfast stance – often parenting on her own. *Autism, Are you F*&^ing Serious?* Will make a deep impression on all readers, but if you have a child who is "on the spectrum" this book is a godsend.

CONTENTS

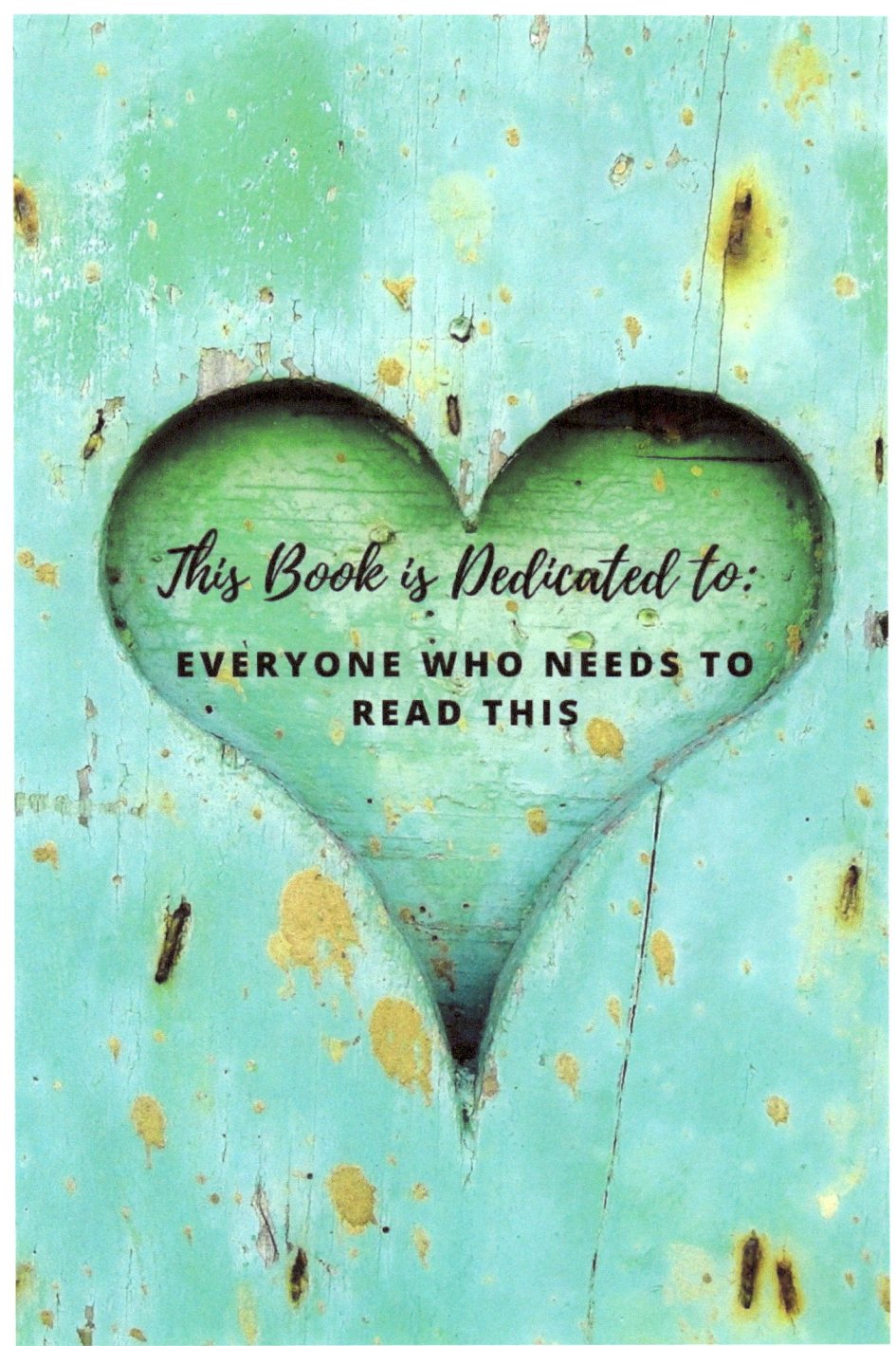

This Book is Dedicated to:

EVERYONE WHO NEEDS TO READ THIS

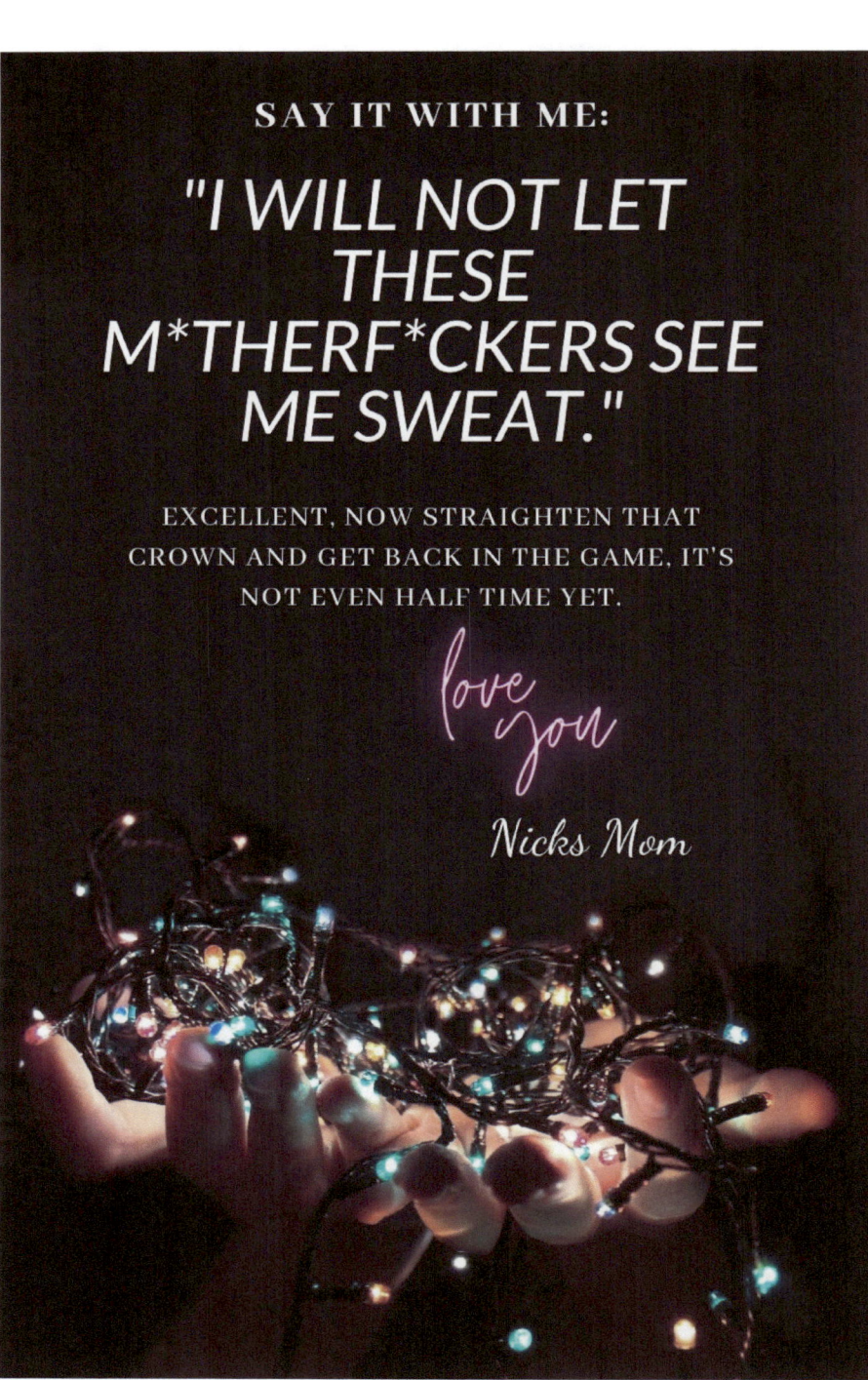

SAY IT WITH ME:

"I WILL NOT LET THESE M*THERF*CKERS SEE ME SWEAT."

EXCELLENT, NOW STRAIGHTEN THAT CROWN AND GET BACK IN THE GAME, IT'S NOT EVEN HALF TIME YET.

love you

Nicks Mom

"It was the tiniest thing I ever decided to put my whole life into."

Terri Guillemets

DON'T JUDGE ME.
YOU HAVE NO IDEA
WHAT WE HAVE BEEN
THROUGH –A PREFACE

◆ ◆ ◆

A friend of mine read the title of this book and said, "I can't wait to hear how this title came about." And I realized, I wrote nothing in this book about why I made my title so profane. Other than profanity catches the eye! I think the words, "Are you F*&king Serious?" have come across my lips more than any other phrase since I had my son 13 years ago. The only other expression I used to say more was, "F*&k My Life" but I had to stop saying that, because I felt like every time I said that, the universe took it as a challenge. But, what better way to get another parent's attention? BAM! Autism disorder inspires this hypothetical question we all mutter, and we aren't really looking for an answer.

I want everyone who reads this to know I am a regular person and I have no special powers. I am not rich, and I am not astoundingly intelligent, but I am gifted in a few ways – nothing you also couldn't be skilled at with a little perseverance. I am asked a lot, "How do you do this?" and I am going to *guess* that means, "How do I continue to live my life with my autistic son who is six feet tall, 300 lbs. and is sometimes very violent?" And I have a simple answer every single time, "Love, that's *how*." I love my son. He is who he is, and I have come to realize he defines me, now. And I will discuss that more in this book; but I am now on a trajectory to fulfill enough of my destiny in my lifetime so that Nick might have a better quality of life in the years when I am no longer here with him.

We have been to hell and back together and I am hoping this account of my and Nick's journey will prevent at least some heartache, undo some myths, and unveil some truths. After all, this is written by a Mom, for Moms and Dads, and every single thing I learned along the way, I struggled to find, and even more so to accept. Please, don't judge me as I tell you the most raw and sensitive story I have ever told – my own.

I hope we can laugh and cry together, and I trust you will be stronger for reading this. My aim is to empower you with knowledge. Now let's get to it. This is going to be something.

01 SO, YOU HAD A BABY?!

First of all, I want to congratulate you. You have passed over the threshold from daughter to mother, or son to father. This new title does not come easily and lightly. This is the hardest most thankless thing you will ever do. No one will tell you that some days are just terrible – the entire day. But being a parent isn't always terrible. I have one son. His name is Nicholas and he was diagnosed with autism just before he turned two. I was not married; I was 21 years old and I was not ready to become a mother. The title was thrust upon me – how much this would change the entire course of my life, I had no idea! I gave birth to another human! It's exhausting; let's all sit and cry about how tired we feel. Sigh... OK, that's over, I think dinner needs to be stirred.

That's what it felt like didn't it? Like you just did this hugely profound thing, and the frickin' pot of spaghetti sauce still needs stirring?! I was so mad and sad and frustrated having my son, I didn't stop and just take in the fact – I had a whole human being inside of my womb, growing, and then I brought him into the world, to live. I was in some huge rush to get back to my "normal" life, and I was not in the state of mind to be a Mom. I was too young, too inexperienced and, to be honest, I was not a huge fan of kids. It always seemed easy enough to babysit and make sure the kid was fed, and had a bottle. But actually, providing that food and bottle, and never giving the baby back to someone was the most insane and incredible thing all at once!

Whoever thought it was a good idea to call me an adult at that age was sorely mistaken. But there I was, with a baby. Looking back, if I had known what I was up against, I don't know what I might have done. You just can't fathom the ways your life changes as a parent, but when you become a special needs parent your life transforms exponentially, and is never the same again.

What is autism exactly, you may be asking? Well, a lot of people will say it is a neurodevelopmental disorder. Some will say it is genetic, some say it is due to vaccines, and then you have people who talk out of their ass and will say it's any number of things, but the truth is, no one knows for sure what autism actually is. All we know is based on what we can see and measure. So, built on a number of specific characteristics that we can measure, a child or person is diagnosed with autism and put on the "spectrum"; in other words, on a scale of severity.

No one ever flat out told me that my life was about to turn into something closely resembling a movie on the Lifetime channel! No one told me that my family would judge me for things I did, and did not do. No one told me I would lose most of my friends because my son was not "normal" enough to play with their children. And what no one told me, I had to learn through many awkward interactions.

People don't want to say it out loud, but they are afraid of what they don't know. Most parents would rather distance their child from special needs children – behaving as if they could catch a mental disorder through interactions, rather than seeking a deeper understanding for themselves and their children.

They won't admit that the way your child hums or fidgets is annoying to them, not necessarily to their children, and they might even flat out lie and make up some crazy reason why your child shouldn't go to, or wouldn't enjoy the event they planned. Just know, it's OK. You don't want those people in your life, TRUST

ME. I had so many "friends" before I had Nick. I watched some of the "coolest" people I knew become very ugly to me. You will see very quickly how judgmental the world is, and how some people will say the meanest things, ask the most stupid questions, and for the sake of what we are talking about, be the dumbest people you have ever encountered.

Remember that Lifetime movie I was talking about? Yeah, so everyone who saw that movie will give you plenty of advice on your life after knowing you for 30 seconds. They'll tell you, with a straight face, the entire plot about this one girl who built herself some machine and ended up being some super-genius, so you're going to be "OK". They will quote myths like firm truths and put their hand on their heart and say that they "know what you are going through," or "know a lot about your hardships" because they once met someone with autism.

Now, please understand this is not me bashing on Temple Grandin, or anyone who has been through this same struggle. Her movie was *fascinating,* her story *inspiring*, but her *struggle*? *Was unique to her*. It was a long and arduous battle between many different factors that were not covered in a 90-minute movie, and Temple's story took place in very different times than now, some 40 years ago. I am not cold, and I am not being mean when hearing someone else's story – I have learned to validate it and appreciate it for what it is, but I understand their story is unique to them. You can draw similarities in a lot of autistic children and people, but they are all very truly different. In the entire world of nearly eight billion people you would never find the same two absolutely atypical individuals; so, to assume autistic individuals are anything other than individuals sets you, and your little one, up for failure.

As you learn to be around your autistic child, it is most important to judge them on their own milestones. Placing the same expectations on your autistic child as on other kids in his or her age group might set you both up for failure or disappointment. Be sure you are basing their growth against their individual capabilities – not what everyone else thinks they "should be doing". Do this and you will already be leaps and bounds ahead of me and my family when we started on our path to learning about the vastly different ways a child with autism develops in comparison to atypical children.

"Face reality as it is... Not as you wish it to be."

Jack Welch

02 SOMETHING SEEMS...OFF...

When I say "something" I actually mean – pretty much everything. Everything was "off." From the very beginning, Nicholas was so different to any other baby I had ever been around. He slept for only two hour increments twice a day, for months and months. He didn't sleep through the night for more than seven hours; sometimes he would break it up into three hours, then get up for 17 hours more. He was never one to be swaddled, held closely, or put in any kind of child-holder device. Car seats were, to him, more like mini torture devices and Nick would scream the entire time he was in one. I would check to make sure he wasn't wet, or hurt, that he was a normal temperature, not teething, not hungry. I would google things to check and the searches would tell me to just let him cry it out.

Nick cried longer, louder, and more frantically than was necessary. Once he cried for four hours straight; by the time I gave in he was trying to make himself sick. Me, my boyfriend at the time, and our parents would take turns sleeping. We would all sleep in shifts because Nick was brutally exhausting and we would be so tired we would beg each other for a break. Most babies are quite enjoyable, especially after a few months. My son was not enjoyable. He would reach for a general area of the room, and no matter what was held up or offered, he'd cry. So, we would let him down to go for the item himself, to "show us" and he would crawl in the opposite direction and go for the most random items that weren't really enjoyable. We had a gigantic fish tank at that time.

This thing was a monster, so we would use an external filter to help get the water back to that pristine flawless look. Every single time this machine was set up Nick would crawl for it. It was loud, smelled bad, and in general was not a toy nor did it look like one. But if Nick saw this thing his obsession was so deep and he'd beeline straight to the machine. The one time I let him just touch it he wanted to bite the tubes, which is gag-worthy enough, but enter the fact he had teeth. I was afraid he would gnaw into a tube and drink fish water. Needless to say, we began having to filter the fish tank when he was gone or asleep. It was *so bad*.

The randomness of the obsessions was the hardest thing to understand, I think. He would scream like a banshee if we took things away that he couldn't have, or shouldn't have. And before you think *every kid does that*, he would then fight us in day-long dragged out tantrums seeking those items out. One tantrum lasted three full days. Every morning, he would wake up, walk to the fridge, open it and try to climb the shelves like stairs, for three entire days. From the time he woke up until bedtime he would fight to get to the kitchen to open the fridge to climb the shelves, and when stopped his screams were so terrifying. I tried to offer him everything on top of and inside of the fridge, showed *him* the top, held him up to *show me*; nothing worked. He would scream like I was trying to boil him alive. I have never heard anything like it before or since. Thank God my Mom took him the next night and he never tried it again.

We began to notice Nicholas was developing physically at a rapid pace, and he was amazing with gross motor skills but falling behind in fine motor skills. He would never do anything involving fine motor skills as he was directed – he would instead throw tantrums.

When your child is not really developing according to the naturally expected progression, such as other babies are developing, it's hard to tell if they are falling behind or if the baby is just not attending to the tasks. Over time it will become very apparent that something seems a little different from other kids.

Some signs to look for in the period up until 12 months of age are:

- Little interest in baby games or songs
- Little to no laughter
- Child seems to look through you, not at you
- No gesturing, head shaking yes or no, pointing etc
- Child doesn't like to be held, cuddled, swaddled
- Little to no verbalisms, babbling or otherwise
- Or the child will have made sounds and babbled, but at the age of forming words (six to nine months) like "Mom" and "Dada" they will instead be very silent, apart from crying for what they want or need.

These are all early signs that your child should be screened for autism. If you feel like your child may have autism it is important to seek out an early intervention program. More on this later!

"Informed decision making comes from a long line of guessing, and then blaming others for inadequate results."

Scott Adams

03 NO, SERIOUSLY, SOMETHING IS NOT RIGHT!

I remember going to the doctor and telling her, "You know, I know I am a new mother, but something feels off." She was very dismissive of my claims as she checked this very healthy baby before her. "Oh honey, new mommies get the baby blues, and sometimes it just feels like the whole world is against you." She picked Nick up and he was happy being turned and held in strange positions, but as soon as she put him down, he began to cry, hysterically, as if she had dropped him. I explained to her that was always his reaction to being put down, even more so when he was in a restraining device like a car seat. I explained that he would scream like we were killing him, and it was worse if he were swaddled. I reiterated all the worries and strange things I was noticing, and she simply said, "Boys will be boys, you get some rest and it'll be fine."

As a new mom, I internalized this "weirdness" I felt with me and my child. What was I doing wrong? Maybe it was me? I stayed away from him when I could, and he seemed happy, but then he would scream and fuss for everyone else. I would dote on him, holding him until I couldn't feel my arms any more, and he would still act so distant from me, and clamor for things out of his reach.

Nick put himself and me in some strange positions by contorting and trying to flip out of my arms.

As the months passed and he grew older, things became worse and worse. I knew something was wrong. I was seeing a different doctor – this time it was a man. At one appointment he checked Nick out for his 11-month visit, gave him a bunch of shots, and I began to explain how Nick's behavior was escalating.

He hadn't slept through the night; he was already walking, but was putting himself in very dangerous places and climbing to scary heights to try and free fall off furniture.

I explained that Nick was talking at one point, then he had stopped, and that he had begun refusing foods that he once devoured. He was not sleeping normally for a child his age, and never had slept normally. It was now my turn to cry hysterically as I explained that I felt like my son was going to drive me insane, or possibly into an early grave. I hadn't slept properly in almost a year. My mother was not available to help because she was helping my grandmother with dementia. Everyone who could help worked full time jobs, but daycare was out of the question. So, between me, my boyfriend and our parents watching Nick in shifts, I was only doing what I knew to do. We were all used to "normal children" this wasn't everyone's first rodeo with children. I had stressed that fact to this doctor. Nonetheless this doctor gave me a pitiful little smirk, and giggled, "Wow, you sure need a break. Why don't you quit your job and just focus on being a mom, 'kay?" I was in tears and pretty tired, but I heard him correctly. He said *quit my job and focus on being a mom.* Because I wasn't focused on being a mother, my son was the way he was. I had been in this office every single month for a year, telling him progressively how my son was not like any other children I had ever encountered, and his response was: focus harder.

I could not feed my son on smiles and love, so I was not actually able to quit my job. Instead, after that appointment I had to take my son home and get ready for work. I went into work that day with my face so swollen from crying I had to sit for almost half an hour before my shift to be able to see. As I sat at the employee bar, one of the cooks came in to get his check. He took one look at me and said, "Hey whoa, are you ok?" I started crying again, and began to blurt out the whole story to poor Patrick, the cook.

I learned something that day: God puts certain people in our paths – they aren't always meant to stay – but they are meant to be there at that moment, and that day God put Patrick in front of me.

He said, "Listen to me, and don't you ever f*cking forget this, if you feel something is wrong with your child, then there is something wrong. Now, there's some weirdos out there that make sh*t up to make their kids sick, but you're not a weirdo, you know your son better than anyone, and if something is not adding up, you don't let anyone tell you different, you seek the answers until you know what's wrong. Here, I have some people you need to call."

Patrick gave me names of three agencies to contact immediately:
- Southwest Human Development (SWHD)
- The Department of Developmental Disabilities (DDD)
- Arizona Early Intervention Program (AZeip)

I called them the very next day, and set up appointments with each agency. They individually came to my home and evaluated Nick for a few things:
- What skills Nicholas lacked
- What services he could potentially benefit from, based on what they observed
- How his disorder affected his daily quality of life
- Southwest Human Development did a "prescreening" and found that Nicholas needed long term care instead of regular state health insurance.
- Each agency advised me Nicholas needed to be formally diagnosed, and *then* he could receive maximum assistance and Social Security benefits.

What they did not tell me, however, was how to access those services, how to get him diagnosed, and what it even meant to be a part of this culture. They were very wonderful and informative, but they essentially just got the ball started – not "the ball rolling", and left us to cope. They gave us no map or navigable list even. We were left to guess.

From the age of 12 months to 24 months there are some very blatant signs of autism that should be immediate red flags for you to seek an evaluation for your child. Some of the signs may include:

- Rocking back and forth while they sit
- High-pitched humming, noise repetition or mimicking random things out loud, or at a very inappropriate volume
- Little to no eye contact when spoken to
- Fidgeting or "stimming" (aka stimulating themselves) with a repetitious act, like spinning, wagging, flipping, flapping items or their hands
- Obsessive placement of toys or items
- Motor skills may seem inconsistent or delayed
- Not picking up on social cues from other kids
- Tendencies to "grab" or snatch things without emotional regard for others
- Constant rearranging things on shelves, or toys in a row etc
- Sensory sensitivities (bright lights hurt, loud sounds scare them, certain textures make them sick)
- Crying for "no apparent reason"
- Disrupted sleep or very erratic sleep patterns
- Not sleeping through the night more than three nights a week

"An Incompetent traitor is no danger. It is rather the capable men who must be watched"

Isaac Asimov

04 DOCTORS WHO AREN'T PARENTS

Storytime...OK, I already know I am going to get so much crap for this, but I am going to say it anyway... Doctors who are not parents should not give parenting advice that they have never applied themselves. There, I have said it! While "Don't shake the baby" is something every doctor has to tell new moms, not all doctors – especially those straight out of medical school – need to tell real life parents how to be a parent – instead, they should listen and observe.

For example, when I was explaining very clearly to my son's physician all the "strange" things he was doing, instead of telling me to quit my job he should have taken the symptoms all into consideration and discussed the case with his peers. He never did that, so when Patrick told me about these three agencies, I called them immediately. When they did their evaluations, none of them could diagnose Nick, but every single one said Nicholas has classic signs of autism. During this period in my life I was dating someone whose mother was a special needs teacher, and she too mentioned Nick was displaying the classic signs of autism, so I did some research of my own.

Nick wasn't displaying *some* signs of autism; he was displaying nearly *every single* symptom of autism! Autism is very difficult to diagnose for some physicians, because not all doctors know what they are even looking for. My son's doctor hadn't a clue about what was wrong, he was grasping at straws and assuming it was me as a mother just complaining about a crying baby. His narrow-minded ignorance and one-sidedness cost us valuable months of time, and I knew I had to find someone to go beyond the authority of that doctor, because I felt it in my bones – something was not right – and it wasn't just in my head.

I researched who can diagnose autism and found that developmental psychologists in the state of AZ were the only professionals who can make that diagnosis so early. At the time, finding a developmental psychologist was like finding a leprechaun. So, I had to convince Nick's doctor – who was convinced it was all in my head – to send us to a very sought-after specialist. I won't lie, that day in his office I used my very large stature to become extremely intimidating, and I wouldn't leave without the referral. So, while Nick's primary care physician (PCP) is berating me about the referral, he had the audacity to say to me, as he is handing me the letter, "Let him tell you how wrong you are, and you can come back and tell me how right I was." I am not making that up – that is a verbatim statement this doctor made to my face.

When I set up the initial assessment with the developmental psychologist it turned out to be for a series of appointments that were going to take several hours each. I was asked to be prepared to literally be there most of the day while the doctor would be sitting with Nicholas and evaluating him. This made my nerves all jolt; a doctor would be assessing my child for real – in his *raw* nature – *without* me? *Yep.* He had his secretary tell me to bring a book or a game and just let my son wander as he evaluated him and asked him to play or do certain tasks. I had never let Nick down out of my lap in a doctor's office before, because he would run, and run fast. He wouldn't stop running and was, in fact, always in motion. From the crack of dawn until the time he was asleep, from the moment he learned to crawl and walk, he was on the move. So, I wasn't that mom. I wouldn't let my little hellion-terror of a child cut a rug and just run like a wildling! I was the mom juggling him in my arms trying to redirect his attention away from being let down to explore.

So, after the three-month wait, a 52-page pre-evaluation parent assessment questionnaire, and virtually no sleep the entire week leading up to the appointment, I was needless to say very anxious going in to see this developmental psychologist. Mainly because I felt like he was going to look at me and laugh and say something dumb, like, "This is just how kids are." Then I would have to drive into oncoming traffic – just kidding – but that's what it felt like, as far as how badly I needed answers on my child's condition. So, on that long-awaited day I nervously signed in, and might I add the Mean Girl of my middle school was the office manager! This felt like a bad omen, but I was cordial, played nicely, and introduced my squirming screaming and very fidgety child, and she immediately said, "Well, the doctor will see Nick now."

My arch nemesis, the Queen Mean Girl herself came lurching out from behind a huge wooden door and lovingly wrapped her talons around Nick's little hand. He toddled off with her, breaking free, running off to a far opened door as the first door slammed shut in my face. I felt tears welling up, I was alone and scared, and I had no one to call. I know my mom will read this and say she would have come, but sorry mom, I asked and this was one of those times Nan and her spells had you on edge, and you had to deal with that. I will never hold these moments against anyone, that was my struggle to deal with, but I felt so terrified and alone as that door clicked shut. There's only one other time I have ever felt that way, and it was years down the road with Nick again at a hospital.

I sat in the waiting area. I couldn't read, I couldn't look on the internet at anything, all I could do was stare at a clock. There was another mother there, who had a child about Nick's age, who was sitting quietly watching a tablet, next to her. I have been in so many waiting rooms, I know I remember this one well because the appointment was so important, but I also remember it being the first time I compared my son to a stranger's child and being angry, as if I had been cheated out of something. For a split second I was mad at this mother for having a well-behaved child sitting quietly and patiently to see a nutritionist.

As I was lost in thought about how easy her life must be, another office staff member came out and yelled my name. I didn't move. She yelled again, "Nick's mom." I snapped out of it and realized, that was me, "Yes!" I stood and approached her, "The doctor will see you now," I was confused. I was told this would take four hours. Immediately I knew this wasn't going to be good. I walked in and Nick was under an examination table with blocks. The doctor was at his desk and he called Nick's name. Nick did not respond.

The doctor said, "Hello, Mom." I sat and greeted him, "Hello, Doc." He sat up and pulled his chair close to his desk, "Well, I have something to tell you." I cut him off and asked, "Are you done for today?" He said, "Yeah, we are done." I said, "What is it? What do you need to tell me? Please don't say quit my job..."

His face contorted, and his brow rose, "Why would I tell you to quit your job? What do you do? Is it bad?" I said, "No, but the last doctor told me that Nick is like this because I need to focus on being a mom." The doctor's face went blank, and he shook his head, "What was that? He said what?" I repeated myself. He looked a little shocked, "Oh, well that is very unfortunate. No, Mom, you don't need to quit your job, but I do need to inform you that your son has a disorder called autism. He in fact has the most classic form of autism, and I would need a little bit of an occupational therapist's evaluation but I can almost guarantee he is experiencing sensory delays and sensitivity."

I nearly yelled, "OH THANK GOD!"

The doctor raised his eyebrows again, and said surprised, "Well, that's not a reaction I am used to getting!" and I had to explain my reaction. Up until then it was all down to me. I was at fault, people were looking at me as if I was the root cause of this child's issues, and no one would listen. Patrick was right, I knew it wasn't in my head, and for the first time I had a formal answer. It was not a good answer, but not knowing is worse than having a root cause. After Nicholas was formally diagnosed, I had to go back and see his primary care physician, and the developmental psychologist gave me a packet on how to diagnose autism for the Southwest Autism Research and Resources Center (SARRC) complete with a checklist of red flags to watch out for when screening a child for autism.

So, I made the appointment to follow up with the PCP, and I made sure to go alone. I sat for over an hour and finally when that doctor came into the room, he immediately asked "Well, where's the li'l guy today?" to which I replied with another simple question, "Sir, do you have children?" He said, "Well no, not yet." I then asked, "How many children have you taken care of?" He said, "Well none, but I don't know what that has to do with anything?" And it was right then I knew I would never take my son to a doctor who was fresh out of medical school, and not a parent themselves. "Well, doctor, it has everything to do with everything," I said calmly, "Remember how I was supposed to come and tell you how right you were about Nick? Well I have come bearing a gift. Here, this is from Nick's developmental psychologist. It's a packet on how to recognize the early signs of autism. My son is developmentally disabled, severely developmentally disabled." He smirked, tossed the file on the counter and said, "Well, now you know huh?" I wanted to throw him down the elevator shaft on his head!

I was so angry we never went back, and I filed a formal complaint against him. If you don't believe anything I have written, please believe this: You can read about brain surgery and in theory learn everything from the neurons to the dendrites, to the way the entire brain looks on paper; but until you cut a brain open and experience the surgery you cannot anticipate what the reality of it is. This is the same thing for parenting. Except we aren't "practicing" parenting, we get one shot – do or die. They are "practicing" medicine, remember that. They are humans, not gods, and you always have the upper hand, never let a doctor determine what is right for your family.

Never Let Anyone Steal Your Shine

-Nicks Mom

05 DIAGNOSES: NOT FOR THE FAINT AT HEART

As you can tell from my story so far, getting a diagnosis for your child might take some time, and be somewhat of a battle. I literally dressed in a white muscle shirt, dickies and boots and offered to handle the situation like gentlemen in the parking lot with his PCP. I do not, and am not, advocating violence but I was a young and angry mama bear who was being ignored and my son and I were treated badly. It was not down to my failures as a mother – Nick had a real condition. I would have fought someone had it come down to it – that's just me being really honest (and a little bit country-raised)!

didn't know any better, I didn't know there were laws on my side, second opinions, helpful advocacy groups like Raising Special Kids, SARRC, Light it Up Blue, Autism Moms, etc. to turn to and ask questions, I will say this so many times in my life – you don't know what you don't know. No one in my family had autism and I was never around children with autism. As an adult with OCD, looking back I might have been a little on the spectrum myself. As far as being educated on early child development, I knew that kids crawled, walked, weaned from bottles, potty-trained, and somehow learned to talk along the way. Most kids are simple:

just feed them, keep them out of danger, make sure they are clean and they will be fine. Most people see raising kids this same way, and so when Nick was diagnosed, this drew a line in the sand for everyone.

I would mention to friends that we finally figured out what was going on with Nick, and as soon as we mentioned autism, we may as well have said "terminal cancer." People were so blatantly cruel and unknowingly rude that it was apparent to both me and my partner at the time, that we were black sheep at best. People stopped answering phone calls, and wouldn't come over.

I spoke briefly in the beginning of this book about what autism is, and how we really don't know where the disorder itself comes from – nor has there ever been a definitive explanation in regards to the source of the condition. Scientists don't know if it's purely genetic, or if it is environmental, or indeed a culmination of the two. All that is concrete about the disorder can be measured in social interactions, lack of self-control and several other verbal and non-verbal communication delays that are all relatively common among all divisions of the spectrum. While it was once thought that autism meant your child was like the main character in the film "Rain Man", there is so much more knowledge now, and the depth of understanding to this disorder has evolved into a more modernized formal awareness of the spectrum. There are now believed to be not just one blanket disorder of autism, but five different levels or categories of autism, and they are:

- **Classical Autism:** shows classic symptoms by age three
- **Pervasive Developmental Disorder (PDD-NOS):** shows several signs and behaviors of autism but doesn't meet the criteria for classic autism
- **Childhood Disintegrative Disorder (CDD):** also called Heller's syndrome or disintegrated psychosis; this is a rare form of autism where the delays are later onset rather than early, and sometimes can be noticeable by severe reversal in skill levels

- **Asperger's Syndrome:** is thought to be the lowest form (highest functioning) of the disorder, children with AS usually display poor social skills, they are very repetitive, firm in their beliefs and viewpoints to the point of being unyielding, and they are focused on rules and routines.

- **Rett's Syndrome:** until recently this was not recognized as an autism disorder; it is now defined under the spectrum and most usually affects girls more often than boys. It is a genetic disorder that essentially leads to the deterioration of even the most basic skills likes crawling, walking and eating.

We had so many family members telling us what to do, how to do it, coming at us from all angles. Nick was insatiably seeking out danger at this time. He would smash windows with his hands, and head. He would jump from the tallest heights and dive to the floor on his head. He would hold burning hot lightbulbs until his flesh would melt and we had to remove all accessible lamps and replace them with ceiling lights. Then he was flooding the house several times a night, or his favorite thing to do was to get up very quietly and shut our bedroom door, then run around and trash the house, take everything out of the fridge just to leave it all on the floor.

We would wake up to the entire house trashed and flooded, all our food spoiled and Nick would be back to sleep or he would be in the tub letting it run over as he splashed and floated. He loved ice cold water, and his grandpa was so scared of this he taught Nick to swim at six months old. From then on Nick was obsessed with water. We would explain this to our parents and tell the doctors, and everything was linked back to "He's autistic." We had to begin locking him in his room, setting alarms to check in on him, putting steel door grating over windows, the kind one would use on the bottom of a door to prevent a dog from scratching the door up. We replaced all windows with Plexi-glass and even had to go as far as moving into our own place just so we could reinforce the walls with plywood, carpet and padding. It felt like we were slowly being locked into our own prison or routine and drone-like schedules. No one wanted to come around us, we never were able to travel and we ended up isolating ourselves from even the people who did stick around. It was unhealthy and it is not something I suggest you do. Had I known there were so many supports I would not have allowed my personal life to dilapidate into what it became.

My partner and I became very angry people who lashed out at one another, we yelled, spanked, and even tried all the methods our parents used to correct our behaviors. I want to say it's because it was all I knew, but it all felt so wrong. I was raised in a very stern household and I never wanted that to also be the way I parented, but it became the only way I knew how to be. I was holding Nick to a standard that others were holding me to, and it wasn't fair to him. We went down some very sad roads because we as the parents were unaware – we were the very problem – it wasn't the autism. We were terrible because we didn't know we were terrible. I regret it, I am sickened by it, I think about all the times of nasty yelling and screaming, and physically trying to intimidate him. It was all the "old stops" and we tried only what we were armed with. So, I am going to provide a few do's and don'ts right here that will help you skip *YEARS* of trauma and sadness.

Tips for Autistic Children under the Age of Five:

- Do not hit, spank, and/or yell at your child in anger. They will learn this is how to get what they want, and that anger is how to communicate need.
- Do not pay attention to small nuisances or "annoying" behaviors, instead wait for them to stop and then ask them if they need something. Show them the way you prefer they communicate with you by way of example.

- Try *AS MUCH AS POSSIBLE* to keep your cool. Autistic children sometimes seek attention in negative ways because they know no better – the more you attend to them during these times, the more they are going to revert back to this behavior in the future when they want something – so remain calm.

- Talk to them directly, using easy and specific vocabulary. Do not be general and say things like "pick that up" and point in a general area.

- Use words specific to what you want, "Nick, pick up the red toy car, please". Being specific will help them understand you and what you are asking, the first time.

- Give the child clear expectations of what is to come using "first and then" language. If my child wants to do something, but I need him to do something first, I structure the conversation to outline both activities in a way that we will both get what we want. Example: Nick wants to watch TV but I want him to brush his teeth, when he points to the TV, I say "Great job asking for TV, but first you have to brush your teeth, then you can watch TV." This gives him clear expectations as well as validates his want.

- Build your team. Find people willing to get in the weeds and do services for you and with you. Nick's main care provider is the Captain of my high school football team, and a navy veteran. You will be surprised who is willing to say "F*ck it" and roll up their sleeves and do the hard work. *SO*, find at least *ONE*.

Figure out what services your insurance and the local government offer for special needs children or early intervention programs. These services will change your life.

Each service is unique from the other and you are usually going to work through a case worker or case manager to get these services. They are typically paid for by the state (if you aren't rich) and are given to the closest person caring for the child (grandparents or whoever is the "parent" figure). These are just some of the assistance programs that you may be offered as a guardian of the special needs' child:

- **Respite Care** is basically time for you to go and be a normal human, while being certain there is a qualified care provider there with your child to make sure they are safely supervised. Think state-certified, FBI-fingerprinted "babysitters".

- **Habilitation** is going to be a set of goals you create for the child, and the care providers have to help the child achieve these goals. Hand-washing, toileting, picking up toys, learning how to obtain new skills, etc. Think of an "in home tutor" for this service.

- **Attendant Care** is a service that is provided in the instance a parent cannot do something with the child on their own. Bathing, transitioning from one place to another, making meals for the child, doing light chores to maintain the household (common areas that the child uses) Think "assisted living" for this service.

- **In-Home Nursing Care** is something you can get if your child has wasting syndrome, or is presenting issues with feeding, taking medications that are vital to living, and other life and death issues that might require medical attention either daily or a few times a week.

- **BCBA (Board Certified Behavioral Analyst)** and **ABA (Applied Behavior Analyst**) are services that help with learning about why your child is the way they are. If your state does offer these services, I will be honest and say these are the best, most life-changing services you can get in home. This were the services that most helped me as a parent.

Yes, you can receive all these services on top of each other! And yes, you can absolutely ask for more hours if you need more, but you must present the reasonable need for more. Say you become a student and need 12 more hours for going to school, you might be able to get that extension if you present your official schedule to the case worker.

To be completely transparent, until I learned about what behavior really was, how consequences, punishments and everything in between worked, I was not doing anything good for my son other than sustaining his life, and the quality wasn't that great. We were isolated and safe. That was about it. Until I as a parent began to take training, accept that what I knew was not enough, and stepped outside of my own preconceived notions of who my son should be, I was not effective at getting anywhere with Nick. We operated out of fear, anger, sheer exhaustion and complete ignorance if I am being scarily honest with myself.

"The first step is you have to say that you can"

Will Smith

06 NOW WHAT THE F*CK DO I DO WITH THAT?

That last chunk of information, the diagnosis of Nick with autism, was a lot to take in, so it's OK to take a deep breath and cry a little. Crying helps – but only in small amounts; too much crying will make you feel at liberty to cry, and well, if I gave myself the green flag to cry, I might not ever stop, so be careful. Do feel sad when you need to, but don't feel desperate, alone, pathetic – none of that now. I'm serious – don't do it. You are doing your best with the cards you were dealt with and to quote a very dear friend of mine, "they want to talk about the life I lived, but they haven't lived it," and it's so true. The only person who can truly gauge if you are OK, is you. If we are frank and sincere, no, none of this is OK, but you have to be at one with the reality of your situation. What you are facing is not a sprint, it's a long, long marathon; if you judge yourself based on what others say, feel, tell you to do, and want you to do, you will drive yourself crazy. I know from experience; I have done it.

So, what the f*ck do you do with all this information? What do you do once you have fought the doctors to believe you – and now they do – and your child has a "label"...Now what?

Yeah, they didn't tell me that either. They waited for me to navigate services I had no clue existed. Services that were not explained to me in a bullet-pointed presentation (see Chapter 5 for the list of services that exist in most states) – they were sent to me in five gigantic stuffed envelopes! All the envelopes were filled with spreadsheets listing services and their phone numbers. And the services themselves were named in acronyms (OT, SLP, BCBA, ABA etc.). Each envelope was vastly different (some really thick, one really thin, one was only one page), but the lists explained nothing about what the service was – it was just a database of phone numbers. I didn't have any clue what that meant – was I supposed to call these people? Would they be calling me?

Do I call the closest ones? Literally, not a single direction was given in the envelopes. They were from the Department of Economic Security of Arizona, the Developmental Disabilities Department, but with no salutation so I wasn't sure who to call. I know now, this was a lack of training and understanding on my caseworker's part. She should have called me, discussed each service that existed, vetted each service with me for its potential benefit to Nick, then sent me lists of agencies that are available to provide those services, and ONLY those services. She did not do that; she did not call and introduce herself, and she also did not speak English as a first language so immediately we had several communication barriers. I am not someone who automatically believes that because someone cannot speak good English, that they are not intelligent. Instead I tried to find a better way to communicate with her, so I began to send emails because I couldn't understand her on the phone.

She began to send me nasty voicemails saying it was my lack of understanding her – not her lack of communicating – that was creating barriers. This went on for almost a full three months before I realized she must have a supervisor I could speak with. The supervisor I finally spoke to adamantly stated that my son's case was a high needs case, but was not being treated as such. I had been accidentally filed into the "less severe" side of the autism cases in that division. I was not supposed to be in that department which provided low attention caseworkers! The lady I was having trouble speaking with was taking it so personally that she wouldn't take the time and look at the amount of services Nicholas needed to be evaluated for.

I am telling you this story because this was when I realized that these services lived and died with me – I was the only Captain in the ship who was in the ship 24 hours a day, and if I didn't take that helm and steer this ship, we were going down in a cove of rocks. Never wait for people to explain things to you when it comes to your child – interrupt, ask questions and do not move on until you fully understand what is being explained. I was young, I was bullied because I was a new mom, and I was even more bullied because I was a young mom with a special needs child. So, as you read this, I am handing you a power no one gave me, but that I had to discover. You as the parent can say and ask whatever you choose, as long as it's not a threat to anyone. You can tell them to slow down, stop using big words, you can ask for an interpreter, you can have a family member with you or friends, you are able to ask Google in the middle of a meeting "what does this mean?" Yes. Be that person, because if you aren't that person no one else will be. You are the Captain and you are not to be swashbuckled!

If your child's name is on something, you have the right to see it. If you are part of the conversation – in most states, you can record it. (Check the legalities of that for your state but in Arizona it's true). When someone writes up recommendations for your child, ask who wrote it, how long they evaluated your child, and what did they use to come to their conclusion? Is it an arbitrary system they decided on, or is there a measuring scale, if so, what is it? Ask them to show you.

You see, you may not even care to know, but the fact that you ask sets you apart from 90% of parents who sit quietly and nod their heads as some faceless state official, or a doctor who never looked at their child, decides the quality of the child's life and the amount of care they need. Yes! That happens. Some doctors have clinicians doing the evaluations and they are writing whole release orders, and dictating families' entire worlds when they leave that facility – using second- and even third-hand notes from student doctors, physician's assistants, and people simply NOT qualified to make these life-altering observations and decisions.

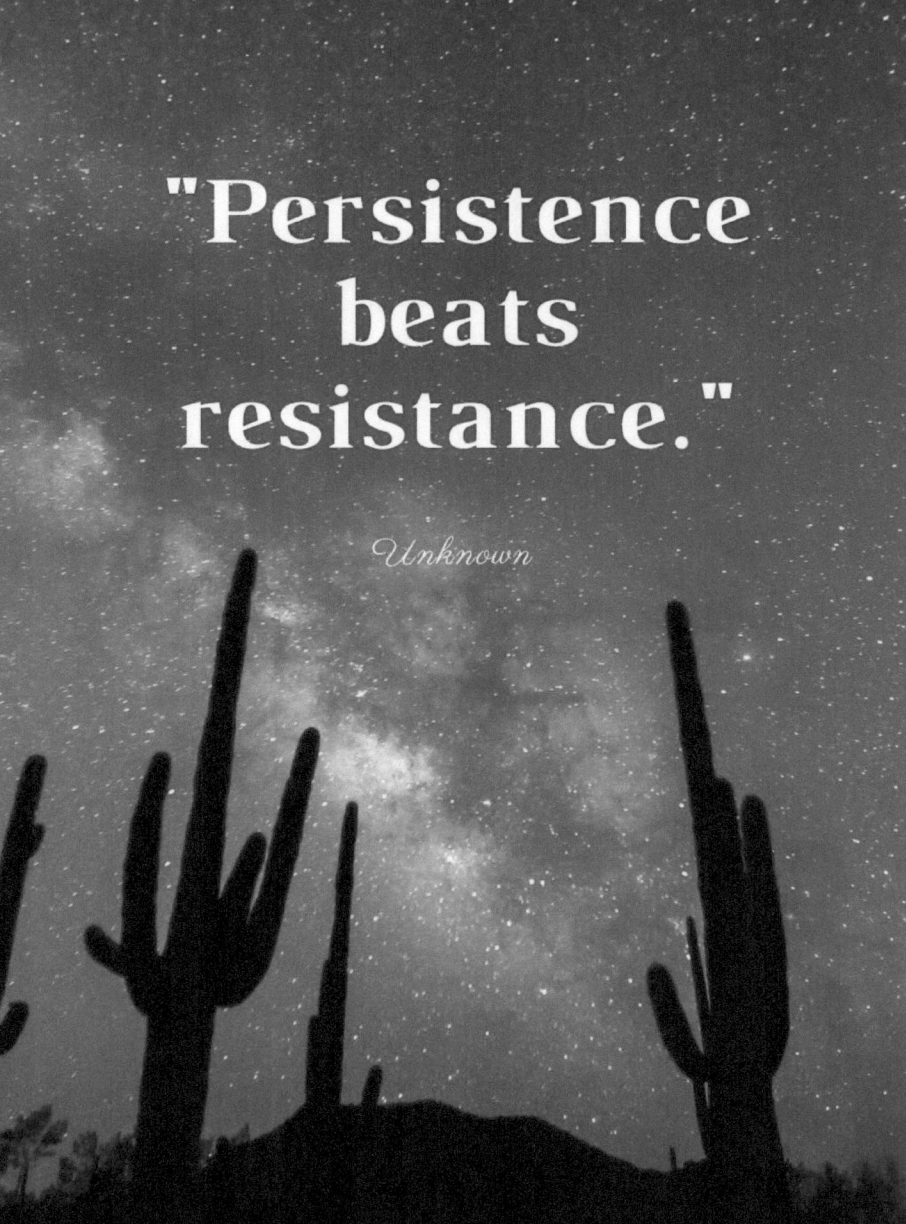

"Persistence beats resistance."

Unknown

07 THERAPY, YEAH! THAT WILL WORK... SOMETIMES.

L et me preface this chapter with a very important statement and question: Therapy will only give you what you
want to get out of it. So, what are you willing to sacrifice to
get what you want?

Sacrifice is such an oddly unique word. It has so many meanings
– some of those meanings can have really negative connotations,
but the sacrifice I'm speaking about in my question requires both
profound change and a lot of honesty. It's the kind of honesty it
takes to live in one's truth and know one's limitations. The very
boundaries you "can and cannot" live by are not actually the same
as the boundaries you "will and won't" live by. Nick taught me
this, and it's the most quintessentially simple, yet deep concept.
If you tell yourself you can't, you are correct. If you tell yourself
you can, you are correct. Why are both statements true? Because
you are the one who holds the determination behind the intentions of your actions. If this doesn't make sense, let me explain.

For the longest time Nick would come into the kitchen, reach
for the cookies (we kept them in a cabinet above the fridge at this
time), and because he was unable to reach them, he would ask for

help. Well, it would be right before bedtime or before school, and I would use his height limit to my advantage and deny him access. The only reason he "couldn't" get those cookies is because he was looking at the situation as "Dang, I can't reach them, so I can't have them if someone else won't get them for me." It only took a few times of him asking me at the wrong time, and being denied, that he finally said to himself, "Hmm Mayyyybeee I can get to them?"

And this is actually how all minds work. We set our own limits and most of our "can't" inner talk is someone else using your limit to keep you where they need you. After so many times of me telling him no, and being shut down, he used the determination of his intentions to get those cookies to change his "can't" into "will". He got his largest truck, turned it on its side, took his little leg and lobbed it onto the counter, he pulled himself up on the lower counter, walked over to the taller counter, stepped up and the used the toaster to step on and get to the cabinet with the cookies. He earned those cookies!

It was this very simple concept and idea of the power of inner talk being so important, that made me realize the power of the things I do with Nick are just as profound to his development as the things I don't do, or wasn't doing.

We foster two emotions more than any others when in the role of parenting – these two buggers are: love and guilt. Love for our children, and the guilt that can arise for a multitude of reasons; mine personally comes from what I didn't do for my son, sooner. I regret not structuring my home and living a little more honestly with myself, sooner. I lied to myself for a long time. I'll admit I was once in the same category of parents who said, "We do all we can," but deep down I knew I was just handing my child to professionals and teachers most of the day and hoping they would just "fix" my son. I think it was a mixture of needing to check out of reality to just get through the day, and I didn't really see the progress I wanted to see.

There was one care provider who sat me down once after

realizing I was lukewarm about every single thing the intensive therapy providers were doing. He said, "Listen Mom, if you don't think what we are doing is worth the time for you to join in and really buy into to the program, we may as well not be here. We can't just fix the situation unless you are the glue to make everyone follow the same patterns the same program the same way every time. This won't work without your buy-in, period." He said it just like that, and it was the way I needed to hear it. I was clinging to the idea of what I wanted. I wanted my son to be "fixed" but it wasn't Nick that needed "fixing" it was me! I needed to stop clinging to the person I had designed as "my son" in my head, and once I sacrificed the part of me that had the hopes of handing my son car keys on prom night, seeing him study for the SAT's and sharing long road trips for college football, I was able to realize my son was a completely different person to this – but he was still equally interesting and amazing. I still can dream of his accomplishments, but he will determine what those are. As a parent you learn to sacrifice yourself in tiny bits at a time. Children pilfer our youth and return its worth in wisdom. We learn that in our wisest days we know very little, but one very important thing that will be stressed to you from an early stage of your journey with your diagnosed child, by everyone you encounter, is therapy. "Therapy" is an umbrella term for many things. Each kind of therapy focuses on your child's specific skill, or on a specific deficit of skills, using different techniques that will cater to how the child learns best.

There are so many different types of therapies for so many things. Each therapy can be used for several different disorders or ailments. Each child's need will determine the extent of services they receive, and the kinds of therapy each child receives is tailored to their strengths and weaknesses individually. This is very important to remember. Nick was essentially diagnosed as non-verbal, classically autistic, with sensory integration/processing disorder. He has encopresis (unable to control fecal bodily function), and is incontinent (unable to control bladder function). He has avoidant restrictive food intake disorder (he eats only certain foods that all have similar characteristics), and his vision is very poor. So, from the beginning, Nick was assessed for various kinds of relevant therapy. He was found to need speech therapy, occupational therapy, aquatic therapy, and EIBI. Later down the road, as his behavior became violent, we were able to get him into an intensive Applied Behavior Analysis program.

There are many types of therapy that your child can be assessed for, but the most common will be:

- **Speech Therapy**: to assist with vocal communication and swallowing.
- **Occupational Therapy**: to improve and assist with both developing and retaining daily living skills.
- **Feeding Therapy**: to assist with learning to eat, or to eat better.
- **Aquatic Therapy**: to assist with learning relaxation, body awareness, and many other therapeutic benefits.
- **Applied Behavior Analysis**: this is a service but essentially a therapy, that covers:
- **Discrete Trial Training (DTT)**: breaks down the steps of a desired behavior to implement with the child as a step-by-step routine.
- **Early Intensive Behavioral Intervention (EIBI)**: this is for kids under the age of five.
- **Pivotal Response Treatment (PRT)**: this assists children with self-management skills and social situations.
- **Verbal Behavior Intervention (VBI)**: this will focus on helping to improve a child's verbal skills.
- **Equine/Animal Therapy**: using horses or other animals who are trained to be assistance animals to manage behaviors and teach self-soothing skills.

These are all therapies that could benefit your child as you begin to face each of his or her challenges. Each therapy will focus on specific goals. Just a heads up: you might need to go to your primary care physician to get prescriptions for these therapies, but it is nothing out of the ordinary to do this. These are vital services – you should use them as much as they are offered to you so that you can begin as early as possible to implement reasoning, self-help and self-coping skills, as well as crucial developmental skills, like boundary and spatial awareness.

Nick was in EIBI at 15 months old, then speech therapy and occupational therapy soon after that. EIBI was essentially the same thing as speech and occupational therapy. A very nice woman named Regina would come to our house and sit with Nick to read and talk with him, and try to get him to parallel play with her (get him to mimic what she was doing). We would have to put him in his high chair and buckle him in so that he wouldn't run and escape the tasks. It became a routine: Regina coming to the house, doing her interactions with Nick; then we would all go about our day. I wasn't really sure what she was doing, and I really wish I had the presence of mind to ask back then. Because Nick is so severe on the spectrum, I had this bad habit of just sitting back and letting the agencies "do what they came to do" and I never got in their way, or asked what they did – or why – and I always felt just like an outsider to my own child because of the amount of therapy it has taken to get me to even understand what he needs, or how to interact with him without triggering him. He was never able to get into feeding therapy, but we saw several dieticians and nutritionists.

The nutritionists and dieticians have always been a bust. I have yet to meet a dietician that understands the severity of how Nicholas refuses foods. I have explained the situation more than once to more than several people in these fields of expertise and we always seem to have this conversation about "starving him out of his diet". Because autistic people have issues with textures and scents and many other aspects of food that we can hardly understand, most of them only eat select foods – and that is it. I once met a mother who had three autistic children and none of them ate the same textures and foods. One child would eat only white and brown foods, her middle child would only eat cold and crunchy things, and the youngest was against anything red and orange, and would projectile vomit for mushy textures. Nicholas has that same issue: mushy textures make him vomit. So, when dieticians and nutritionists shove piles of information on me and ask me *what I cook? if I know how to cook? and what kinds of foods I prepare*? it is exhausting and I will be honest: this is a battle I have stopped fighting. Their intake packets are sometimes into the dozens of pages to fill out, then when we get to the appointment the doctor has looked at absolutely nothing I have written and I am expected to then recite the entire packet that took me a week to fill out, from memory.

I know how to cook, I cook rather well, and so does every single person in my immediate family. We are all foodies if you will, but shoving a recipe in front of a kid and telling them to eat it or starve might work for atypical children but for us this creates huge explosive behavioral meltdowns that can become violent and dangerous. This is the part that falls on deaf ears each time. We get a soft nod and "yeah it's gonna be tough," but there's no consequence for them. OF COURSE it's going to be tough, thanks for the reminder! Never is there a solution offered as to how we will go about it, or a conversation of what we might try to start. As my Dad would say, they pretty much tell us "Nike that sucker! *Just do it.*" I have no interest in creating more violent behaviors for Nick, so in this whole situation I'll quite honestly admit, I have no suggestions, or magic rabbits to pull out of my hat. We are still struggling with Nick's food and eating habits every single day. It is now year 13 and we have been advised to give him ungodly amounts of laxative, get him tested further than he already has been and nothing really else "can be done" unless we are up for starving him into eating correctly. I will be honest, I don't physically think we are able to do that at this point, Nick is pushing 6 feet tall and 300lbs. I would worry for our safety if we tried to do this in-home.

We are always hopeful when we have new therapies, and always sad to see the better therapists go. Sometimes the therapies feel like real progress. You see how they go from never being able to match the colors or pictures, to doing it five out of five trials, and it feels wonderful! However, then there are times where the therapies don't work at all. They seem to make your child more angry, more aggressive, and even flat out miserable. When we began occupational therapy, we had an amazing occupational therapist. She ultimately got injured during a session with another child and this was the first lesson I had in the importance of perseverance and autism.

It had taken me several weeks to find this place, it was 20 miles away and the drives were terrible, but we had found this little nook in the world where Nick belonged, and it was epic to see how happy he was to see his therapist. When she was injured and had to quit, it was a traumatic setback. Nick did not like her replacement. We just began speech at the same facility and he was having trouble distinguishing between the two therapies. He loved occupational and hated speech. He would fight and cry so hard and long that it became a waiting game of whether the session would be over before he would quit. It was a nightmare. We stopped going to that facility after our favorite therapist left, and it was back to the search for new therapies and therapists.

We finally found a very new company that was just starting out, and it was amazing! The owner, Lorrie, was the most kind, wonderful and understanding woman. She accepted Nick and was so good about pairing him with talented therapists. The first therapist he had was named Andrea, and I'll be honest, I cried to Lorrie very real, sad tears when Andrea left. It was devastating to watch someone so great with Nick just drop off the face of the planet. As you meet certain people who do these jobs you will find some are truly dedicated to their profession, but you will also meet people who couldn't get any worse if they tried, or care any less than they seem to already. It's unfortunate, but it's the truth, so always be present for the first few sessions to make sure the therapist is tending to your child effectively, and if they aren't, then you have every right to switch providers. You can offer suggestions to help the therapist understand their client a little more by creating a list of likes and dislikes, preferred items and disinterests, and helpful interaction tips – for instance, using certain words or phrases might encourage or discourage certain behaviors more effectively.

In fact, I encourage you to watch the sessions so that you too can pick up on some pointers. I learned something mentioned earlier called "first, then" language. This is, in a nutshell, is the most effective way to transition from their more preferred tasks and environments or objects, to the places, activities, and situations their daily life, and families, require them to participate in. Because autistic minds work differently than the atypical brains of most people we must step back and understand why they "freak out" when asked to do something, or are told to do something. Autistic children and particularly the more severely delayed children like Nick, register sound on higher frequencies and lower frequencies than normal. They can also have higher sensitivities to being sensory overloaded because the processing of information is less "interesting" and more "frightening" because they are so sensitive. I once heard a teenager in Nick's school say he felt like he lived inside a rave party when he was growing up. He thought the outside was too bright and the beams of sun hit him like lasers. He said there were the sounds of the normal outside hustle and bustle, and also the sounds of crackling tree branches with cars zooming by were like the scariest, loudest foreign sounds. He likened the sounds to foreign bombing noises and he had no idea what they were attached to. The consequence of a walk outside was his bloodcurdling screams and his immediate fight or flight response, and it was him fighting for his life, against these frightening foreign sounds.

The average-minded person can assume that if I do *this*, then I can get *this*. You see this with children all the time: *If I pick up my toys, I can go outside and play*, or *If I eat all my dinner, I can have ice cream*.

With children especially it is important for them to know the expectations surrounding their behavior. So, we use *if* and *then* statements naturally to convey the expectations. But the words *if* and *then* (which show consequence or cause and effect in the way they are said) don't register in autistic minds as they do with us. Conditional statements are much like slang to autistic people. The terms of something being conditional is a concept that is hard for normal people to grasp, and exponentially harder for autistic children. If and then are conditional – one is contingent upon the other. So, for example, when I tell Nick "*If* you pick up your toys you can *then* go outside." His mind hears the demand, "pick up your toys" and gets stuck on the fact the demand came without a clean understanding of what *will* come next, not what *could* come next.

So, to avoid this we use "first and then" statements to create a chronological order of expectations. I would instead say, "First you pick up your toys, and then you can go outside." This sentence is clear: one thing will happen first, and then the next will happen. When I first heard this explained it made no sense. "It's the same thing" I remember saying, but once I put it into practice and saw the difference it made to my child – it made sense. It took a lot of buy-in from me and my team of care providers to communicate the way Nick needed us to – not the way that was easiest for us.

Ultimately, therapies only work when you are willing to apply them regularly in the household. One hour a week with a stranger will not fine-tune skills for your child, period. That's just the way it is, these therapists aren't given 20 hours a week with a child, they are given the bare minimum and it is up to you as the parent to decide how relevant the therapies are, how well they are working, and then to foster an adoptive approach to the skills and tasks these therapies are touching on only briefly in sessions. The "first and then" language is only one specific instance of me learning a skill through therapy sessions, but I can promise that's not the only instance when therapy retrained me, more than it was teaching my son. We are all in this situation as blind mice in a maze, and while vast amounts of therapy will improve your child's position in life, it is also there to help better you as a parent. If you are vigilant, present, and curious, therapy can be great for you and your child's skill set.

"Through the blur, I wondered if I was alone or if other parents felt the same way I did – that everything involving our children was painful in some way. The emotions, whether they were joy, sorrow, love or pride, were so deep and sharp that in the end they left you raw, exposed and yes, in pain. The human heart was not designed to beat outside the human body and yet, each child represented just that – a parent's heart bared, beating forever outside its chest."

Debra Ginsberg

08 DOCTOR'S APPOINTMENTS, AKA: THE WAITING GAME

Tick, tock, tick, tock. Seconds ticking down and I always seem to be late for doctors' appointments, and therapies, schooling, and simply just trying to adult! It's a huge tidal wave of too muchness, and drowning or not, I am still expected to be there. You will learn quickly that doctors' offices – all of them, not one or two or every other one, but quite literally every single one – are black holes for time. They give you a prescribed time to be there and if you are late you pay a fee for a missed appointment. My favorite is when you make it in what you think is, "just enough time," but you walk in and beg to be seen, only to be told your appointment has been given away, and the doctor can't fit you in. You will sometimes forget to even make these appointments because hey, your kid is alive and healthy (God forbid!). Then you check your mail and get cute little "reminders" from the insurance company outlining the importance of your child's wellness, the bold and always threatening RED capitalized font urging you to make an appointment – "Today" – as you are sitting down to read your mail at 11pm behind a glass of Moscato.

You will stress out to make the appointment for a time that "sure totally works" on your calendar, but when the time comes, every inconvenient thing to ever occur will happen all at once. Then comes the fight with your child to get dressed, stop crying, stop throwing things, and as they scream bloody murder as you enter the building, the entire waiting room will look at you and wonder what on earth you did to your child to make them holler that loud.

And did I mention your time and your child's time do not matter to anyone in there? While now more than ever it's a complete act of God to get people to do their jobs, doctors' offices have always been code for "hurry up to wait." I am sorry if you are a doctor or nurse but you all move at the pace God gave a snail when it's "not an emergency", and well, we as special needs parents just need a little haste – I know you can't tell, but our whole life is an emergency! By Nick's fifth birthday I would joke I was a professional waiter – not a waiter as in one who brought food and took orders, but a waiter as in I waited, forever. There are a few things you can try to make these situations less abrasive for you and your child.

Here are some tips for doctor's office visits that I wished someone would have shared with me:

- You can pre-advise the office that they need to make special accommodations for a special needs child who will be attending an appointment.
- You can request to be taken directly to a room (not wait in the waiting room) for safety reasons and for your child's wellbeing.
- Ask if there is any preliminary paperwork to fill out and if it can be sent to you to pre-fill.
- You can bring someone to walk around with the child outside or play in the courtyard and you can summon them when they are ready to see you.
- About an hour before your appointment you can fax a reminder or call and remind them you have a special needs child requiring special accommodations coming in for a visit.

- If they are doing several procedures (several shots at one time, a full body exam etc.) you can ask that these procedures be broken down into a few appointments, so as not to overwhelm the child.

I suggest if your child is being inundated by shots (six to eight at a time) to ask that these sessions be broken into more doctor's visits. Yes, that statement makes even me cringe, but I wish someone could have told me that was a little extreme, and that I could say "No – you can do half today or two today and we will come back each week." I was a young mom, and again doctors "know it all", so they shoved information about the dangers of not vaccinating my child into my hands when I so much as asked if "this was a little too much for a baby?" And that was not cool, or OK for them to do, period. This is them, *just doing their job*, I suppose. But it doesn't make it right.

Be prepared to attend several doctor's appointments, they are vital to ongoing services, even if to just document their progress, lack thereof, and their general health. Some things that helped me while attending these appointments are:

- Bring extra people to help wrangle the little one while you fill out paperwork (if you were unable to get the paperwork before the appointment it's hard to fill out paperwork and watch your child so I highly recommend asking someone to help you attend a doctor's appointment where you know you will need to fill out a book of information for the first time).
- I recommend bringing toys and snacks; some parents automatically go for an electronic device, but at a doctor's office it is often frowned upon to have kids on devices due to the noise and data use. However, because Nick is so violent at times and there are times when we need him to sit still for certain exams, we offer him devices then, and only then, so he is more likely to allow the examination to happen. This may be your child too.
- Bring noise cancelling headphones if your child is sensi-

tive to sound.
- Call a few minutes before you arrive at the appointment to remind them of your child's needs.
- If you have paperwork to do after the appointment let the person who is helping you take the child to the car so they can feel they have finished and completed the appointment. This helps Nick to not have any behaviors in the office after successfully attending something as difficult as a doctor's appointment.
- Bring a reward for the child afterward. If they did exceptionally well, give them the reward and be very specific in praising them, "You behaved so well at this appointment, you were quiet and you allowed the doctor to examine you so excellently! Great job on going to the doctor!" Repeat this, it will help reinforce the great behavior that they had specifically that you wanted, and could set the mood for future appointments.

Before you write my editor a terribly worded email that she might correct and send back to you – I am not telling you that doctors are bad, or that they are outside of their job description when they always make you wait, give your child six shots at a time and make you come back 50 times a year, for the first three years of your child's life. But what I *am* saying is doctors are *people*, and not all people are good. Some doctors I have come across have really been amazing and helpful, but a majority has been quite awful to us. Yeah, *a majority*, and that really hurts me to have to say that. I am so polite and so accommodating that I never thought outside of the realm that "Doctors are here to do good." Yes, most are, but some are so set in their own methods and ways that they refuse to seek help from colleagues and it is that pride, and their own issues, whatever they may be, that prevent a patient from getting real help.

My son's psychiatrist once said this to me, and it's stuck with me for so long. He said:

"What do you call the guy who cheated his way through medical school and barely made it out of college with a C average? Doctor. What do you call the guy who studied every day, went to class, and became valedictorian of his class? Doctor. So, Doctor is a subjective term."

Out of the horse's mouth.

"Everyone is a genius. But if you judge a fish on it's ability to climb a tree it will live it's whole life believing that it is stupid."

Albert Einstein

09 SPECIALISTS, WELL AREN'T THEY SPECIAL...

Hopefully you aren't the shy type, because outside of your primary care physician (family doctor) you will need to see a multitude of other doctors called "specialists". They do exactly what they sound like they do – they specialize in specific areas of medical practice. Nick and I saw every single one of these specialists to rule out certain possibilities before seeing a developmental psychologist. Remember I said it took three full months to get an appointment to see the developmental psychologist, so before I saw that specialist, I wanted to make sure Nicholas was healthy in every single other possible way, other than having a development disorder.

We saw all the following specialists within 1 year:

- **Audiologist**: to rule out any hearing issues.
- **Ophthalmologist**: Nicholas had bad vision and we were able to find out just how bad his vision was; the optometrist was not able to effectively assess Nicholas but the ophthalmologist was able to.
- **Gastroenterologist (GI) Specialist:** this is when we

found out that Nicholas was experiencing severe stomach pains from impacted bowels, and encopresis.

- **Neurologist:** we began thinking maybe Nick was having seizures; and because he bangs his head so often, we needed a neurologist to examine him and take scans. Initially it was to make sure he wasn't experiencing any kind of swelling or pain that could be related to tumors or fluid building. We see the neurologist now to look at the effects of his head banging and to make sure it doesn't result in brain damage.

- **Psychiatrists:** these are usually the doctors who help with medications and evaluations for some services to be ongoing; essentially, they determine if the services need to be long-term.

- **Endocrinologist:** will draw blood and determine if there are any kinds of metabolic issues, like diabetes or thyroid abnormalities.

- **Dieticians or nutritionists:** if you are able to work with a feeding specialist or a dietician/nutritionist early enough you may be able to curb some bad habits a lot of moms with autistic children fall into – such as poor and few food choices.

Ruling out any other possible health issues your child may be having, before taking them to the hardest doctor to get to see, is the easiest way to get a definitive diagnosis on the first round of visits to the developmental psychologist. If you don't rule out all these other possible issues first, they will suggest they need checking, and they could leave their determination open until you rule out any other disorder that may be leading to childhood development delays.

Many specialists you only need to see once to rule out some conditions, but a few you may want or have to see at least once a year. Nicholas has ongoing issues that each specialist addresses individually, and building a rapport with each one has helped to establish a good overall understanding of my child's health.

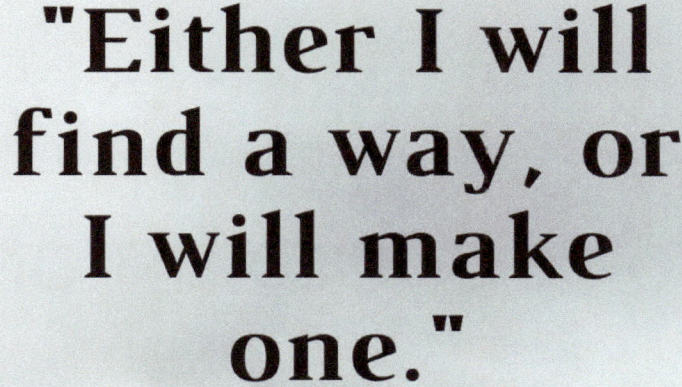

"Either I will
find a way, or
I will make
one."

Philip Sidney

10 THE DARK, SCARY, TOTALLY SH*TTY TOPIC OF MEDICATION

L et's start this whole chapter with a fun fact that we all, as parents of autistic children, should know. Ready? OK.

Fact: There is not one single medication that has been approved for the treatment of Autism Spectrum Disorder.

Did you read that? Read it again. Not ONE. There are several medications used to treat symptoms that come along with people and children afflicted with autism, but for the actual treatment after a diagnosis of autism, there is not one. Why? Because autism is not a disease. A disease is something that needs medication to be cured; a disorder is something we live with and manage. That's the easiest way I can describe it. But there are a lot of medications for a lot of diseases and afflictions that overlap in symptoms, so most of these medications are "off label" or "black label", prescribed to patients with autism for the symptoms they are experiencing. At the age of two Nicholas was prescribed something called Risperdal. This medication is named several different things, but the original medication Risperdal was the first medication we had experience with. Although I did not want Nick on medications, the psychologist insisted this was the only way that Nicholas would ever learn to function properly amongst people, and it would help him sleep through the entire night. So, against my better judgement, my heart of hearts, my gut instincts – I agreed and put my two-year-old child on a medication I had no experience with, had no idea what it was or how it worked; I just blindly allowed a doctor to make yet another life-altering decision for me.

As it turned out, Risperdal was a medication that was not for long-term use, and it was not for children, and most certainly not for long-term use in boys. Risperdal, more well known as Risperidone, was developed for schizophrenia and bipolar disorder and is used to help treat the irritability associated with autism disorder. What I should have done was look up the drug review, taken note of the adverse side effects that Nick could have experienced, as well as look up the long-term effects of the drug, and discuss them with the doctor. Now, I know to do all this, but this was over a decade ago. I was meek, quiet and accepting of anything doctors said back then, something I will continue to advocate against and remind parents over and over: You are the Captain, you decide the course of events – not the doctors.

So instead of doing what I should have done, I just gave the medication to Nick. The prescription stayed the same, without any changes or check-ups for over three months. The doctor never drew his blood, and Nick never slept differently, He was behaving about the same, but sometimes would seem to be in a full-on rage that we couldn't get him out of. We went back to the psychologist, and he gave us an increased dose. That's when Nick gained over 50 lbs in the next six months and I noticed he started to develop what appeared to be breasts. He was chunky but his chest was developing like a 12-year-old female's chest, not a three- to four-year-old male. So, I FINALLY looked into the drug.

The adverse side effects were: sleeplessness, irritability, weight gain, and gynecomastia. All the things I thought he was taking this drug to help with were also side effects of the medication! Enter a separate and really serious side effect called gynecomastia. This disorder is breast and lactation development in little boys due to the blocking of dopamine in their little brains. The medication's dopamine blocking effect stimulates the pituitary gland to produce a hormone called prolactin. Prolactin is what is produced by women during pregnancy to develop breast tissue and lactation.

We were now in the realm of possibly having to go on other medications and this is when I took Nicholas to see the endocrinologist to start monitoring his hormones. When I mentioned this to the psychologist we were seeing, his immediate reaction was to prescribe Abilify. Without seeing Nicholas, based on what I was saying, and the fact that my three-and-a-half-year-old was growing breasts – his immediate reaction was to offer another medication. I was uncomfortable with that reaction so I weaned Nicholas off Risperdal, did not pick up the prescription for Abilify, and I never went back to that doctor ever again.

I spent an entire week reading about psychotropic medications and how they are being used on autistic children. I was not only astounded to see what use the medications were actually developed for, but disgusted to see how they were all used essentially "off the cuff," for autism. There is, and was, and still continues to be no real rhyme or reason to prescribing medications for autism. It is an arbitrary balance between watching the child, measuring the behaviors he or she is developing, and determining whether or not they are having these issues voluntarily or involuntarily. Using observations either first- or second-, and even sometimes third-hand, doctors will prescribe some very toxic medications at what they call "therapeutic doses." These are doses that are the lowest amounts safely tested in adults and sometimes the guessing on dose is left to you as the parent to "play with."

Remember how I first started this book? Did you read the Preface? I said *I am not astoundingly intelligent, but I am gifted in some ways, nothing you couldn't be with a little perseverance.* Well, here are my gifts: I am able to learn things very quickly with little to no instructions, and I can write. So, I knew that if Nick was going to be OK, I mean, really "OK" then I was going to have to dig down, dig hard and learn.

People always say to me, "You are always on your phone," and they would be absolutely correct, but if they paid attention, or asked why, they would learn I am always reading.

I learn very easily. So that means I use every opportunity to read all that I can, all day every day. I wake up and put on my glasses, pick up my phone and immediately am back at learning. I have the entire world of knowledge at my fingertips. So, I have no excuse not researching every medication, it's side effect, what purpose it was originally manufactured for, what the consumer reviews say about using it, and what its long-term user effects are. And that's exactly what I did.

Fast forward seven very long, hard years later, (Nicholas was 10 years old by this time). His biological father was actively coparenting with me on a very real level. We had arranged for Nicholas to go to his house every morning and he would put Nick on the bus to go to school. He began to take Nicholas on the weekends and though we were closing ranks and coparenting well, our parenting skills were lacking. We yelled, ruled our homes with an iron fist, and we both were "wardens" of our households when it came to Nick, but he just got more and more violent. We had no idea what to do but Nicholas was beginning to attack people, he would hurt anything in his way, be it a person, animal or thing, and we all began poorly reacting and the situation finally hit an all-time apex.

One morning we were driving with Nicholas to his Dad's house. The three-mile ride usually took about eight to 12 minutes in heavier traffic. That particular morning it was cold, the windows were fogging and Nicholas was in a mood. In a single cab truck, my boyfriend driving, me in the center, and Nicholas in the passenger seat, Nicholas begins to throw a major tantrum. He kicked the dash and smashed the passenger side a/c vent.

I tried to immediately grab his legs and he kneed me pretty hard in the chest. I began to try to wrap my body around him and stop him from kicking out the windshield (something he has done before). It was one of those mornings, I was not on my game. I was going high, he was aiming low, I was trying to zig and he would zag. He got away from me in this complete freak out moment. He reached past me and grabbed the steering wheel. We went across two lanes of traffic and up onto a sidewalk. We almost hit a biker on the sidewalk but my boyfriend was able to maneuver us back onto the road and we stopped.

Police lights lit up our back windshield, but we were fogged in, Nicholas was screaming and freaking out, and thank GOD, the police lit us up and just drove around us. We sat there as Nick howled and kicked the dash. My boyfriend jumped out – "DRIVE!" He yelled at me as he slammed the door, and ran to the passenger side. He shoved his way into the passenger seat, I slid over and he shoved Nick to the middle; he wrapped his enormous body around Nick and locked him into a hold. "Drive quickly." Nick was screaming and using his head to slam into my boyfriend's chest as hard as he could. He was biting his own arms and ripping his jacket sleeves; when we made it to Nick's Dad's house, he was waiting for us out front.

"I could hear him screaming down the block!" He pulled open the door to retrieve Nick. As my boyfriend handed our very large song off to his father, Nicholas took his Dad to the ground. Let me pause here and detail why this was absurdly a line we had never crossed. My boyfriend in this story is six feet and eight inches tall. He is a monstrously-sized teddy bear, weighing in at 350 lbs – he is quite large. Nicholas's father was six feet four inches tall. He was a varsity baseball player and weighed over 250 lbs. I am six feet two inches tall. I weigh over 300 lbs and I was trained to box, wrestle, and play baseball like a boy.

We are extremely large beings, and my 10-year-old child was tossing us around like we were rag dolls. He almost killed us and a biker, and this morning was a whole new level of anger from Nick, unlike anything I hope you will ever see in your own child. His father went to the floor and my boyfriend immediately tried to help him up and got boot stomp-kicked to the chin. Nicholas was flailing and fighting us like he was in a complete fight or flight reaction, and his adrenaline was so in tune with what he was doing, we were all bruised and battered after this car ride.

That was the first morning we had to take Nicholas to the hospital. His attack was so vicious and so severe, we had no idea what to do. What do you do to a child who will hurt himself and others worse than you could ever even think about doing legally? What do you take away from a child that doesn't care about things, who has no idea of monetary value? Where do you go when you have stuck with "it" and done everything you know how to do, but nothing worked?

You go to the hospital.

And that's where we ended up. The first time was one week. At hospital they wanted to put him on medications that were so noxious and not one single medication was for autism, they essentially said there was nothing they could do unless I allowed them to give him medications freely.

In the state of Arizona, medical marijuana is prescribed rather freely to adults; however, to prescribe medical marijuana to a minor there are only about a handful of reasons or "qualifying conditions," in which any doctor will prescribe it to a child, and not one, but two doctors must sign off on the absolute necessity of use for the minor.

Autism is not one of those conditions, in fact, when it went before a judge, several advocacy groups tried to get autism added to the qualifying conditions in which medical marijuana could be prescribed to a child in AZ, and it was voted down. I tried to get Nick and our sensitive case considered for legislation to view. Because everything is essentially not what you know but who you know (who will kiss someone's ass and who won't) we were not the "right fit for their idea of what it took to sway legislation". The advocacy groups I won't mention, but the political side of why we weren't considered was because each group had cases they were "rallying behind" to be considered for legislation.

When I showed up to a press conference with two of my friends with kids like Nick we were told our cases weren't the kind they were looking for, and we weren't the kinds of mothers these groups could rally for, at which time our children's cases were not only accosted by several groups but we were viciously told to take our cases and deal with them – and that's putting it nicely.

What it boiled down to was we weren't the smiling, stay-at-home moms who had the "community" rallying for us, we were the moms who had to work, weren't on federal or state aid, and we were the moms those groups seemed to hone in and pick apart. We were shunned for speaking freely, and asking questions. Politics, not my thing I suppose? And I really didn't care. I graciously backed away from the legislative side and went to appeal to the science side. But when I mentioned to the hospital that they could begin a study, and even get funding for administering medical marijuana to Nick as an alternative to the very scary cocktail of antipsychotic medications they wanted to give him, the doctor scoffed at me. He said "We don't do that here," and he released Nicholas to us.

Nicholas was so angry at us. He is non-verbal but he can speak with his actions louder than anyone I have ever met. He will hit the walls he walks by and kick them and bang into things and you will hear how frustrated he is based on how hard, and with what body part he uses to make the noise. I wanted to try medical marijuana, an alternative treatment; they said that's not the first line method for treating and/or dealing with such a severe form of autism. But when I pointed out that we have tried a medication that was not actually for the disorder he has, and it failed us; I mentioned the hours of therapy, the structure and schooling, and we weren't successful in any of it. He released us with "on-going services" and directions to take... M Tabs... which is another name for Risperdal.

They hadn't even looked at what I wrote. I plainly, clearly, wrote the amount of trouble we were experiencing due to that medication and we were being instructed by another doctor to take that medication – not even meant for autism – and one that we had already experienced very bad side effects with.

I cried. I sat with Nick's Dad and we hugged and cried. We sobbed so hard and for so long, silently. He finally was seeing what I had been talking about, all of it, finally someone was seeing it through my eyes. "What do we do?" He was so clueless about most of this disorder but in that moment, as a Dad, he wanted to fix something we couldn't unbreak and make perfect. Nick's Dad was a mechanic, so in a man's line of work where he fixes things for a living and when he can't make things better for his only son, he internalizes things. He sank into a deep and dark depression, but we were OK because we were going through it together as a family, and as a team.

Three months later, on a very cold morning in December, after dropping Nicholas off at his Dad's, I got to my office and at the time I was the Assistant to the CFO of a very large sector of the United Way, a global non-profit organization. I would get there very early and make coffee, check the mail and begin my day. Well, this day, I got to work and I put my purse down, went to the kitchen to make coffee and I usually would post a note or funny cartoon to employees every morning so I walked back to my desk and my phone was buzzing. I had three missed calls and five text messages – all from Nick's Dad.

Apparently, Nicholas was told No, he couldn't have a snack cake, and when he began to throw a fit in the kitchen of his Dad's home, they were going into a safety hold because Nicholas started to slam his head into the counter and the wall and anything else he could head butt. So, as they went into the hold; Nicholas used his legs to springboard back and shoved him and his Dad through a glass arcadia door. Thank God the glass was tempered and it shattered into a million pieces. Neither one was cut, but his Dad had to wrestle him in a pile of broken glass like some kind of 90s kickboxing movie. Nicholas was in a full-on rage and his Dad was calling in MAYDAY.

"We fought the good fight, we have to go back to the hospital, please – we have to keep him safe and we have to keep ourselves safe." He was pleading with me and crying. Nick's Dad begged me to come get them right away so we could go to the children's hospital again. My blood was ice cold, I felt numb and I sat for a second and I cried. I cried very hard at my desk in the dark. I didn't even have the strength to get back up and turn the lights on in any of the corridors.

What felt like an eternity passed, and I was able to collect myself. I wrote my boss an email and I still posted the happy meme. I drove to Nick's Dad's house. We sat and talked and Nick was finally calmer, but the mess and the chaos was evident in the pebbled glass sprinkled on his small astro turf-covered patio, and the broken lawn chair. His Dad showed me a fuschia-colored welt that was forming on his arm. As he had wrapped his arms around Nick, Nick sank his teeth into his Dad's bicep. It was bleeding something gnarly. Then he lifted his pant leg and showed me another bite. "He got me twice today, and he NEVER gets me."

His and Nick's face were swollen from crying and Nick, though contentedly twirling a straw he had make-shifted into a pinwheel, was still screeching and rocking. When Nick is agitated, he will begin to make loud noises, scream and hit. When he is coming out of an episode that he might go back into, he will grab an ear and roar loudly, punch himself and rock. He will sometimes seek to get under things or low to the ground and undress himself. These are all signs of distress that he was now showing as his father was talking to me about going back to the hospital. Looking back now, we were feeding into his behaviors and making them worse by talking about him and his adverse behaviors in front of him.

When we returned to the hospital the doctor had a clinician immediately come in and talk to us about our expectations of treatment. She explained that they are limited as far as what they can do unless we are willing to administer medications and allow the doctors to, "do their jobs." We explained that we have used medications before but they led to severe side effects, so as long as I would be able to know what medications they would be administering, and if they would give me enough time to research them even a little bit before just giving them to Nick, then I would agree to let them try a few drugs.

A few medications...

Fun fact number two: using words like, a few, some and several is not definitive enough for a hospital of professional doctors. They will use those words against you in a battle of wits. saying things like, "Well ma'am a 'few' is more than a couple, but not as many as several. And several is more than two, but not many." So, when I made a very ambiguous statement like "we could try a few medications", this was their green light to start experimenting. Do you see where I'm going with this? Be very careful what you say and agree to.

The hospital began to play word games with me, as soon as I gave them the ability to give Nick medications and while I am not particularly skilled in many things, they would soon find out word games were my niche.

Not a single doctor in Arizona, nor a state official, or evaluator, insurance rep, therapist, nor the Attorney General himself was ready for me.

"They weren't looking for a fight. They were looking to belong"

S E HINTON

11 HOSPITALS: WHAT THEY SHOULD NOT BE USED FOR

We were sitting in the 5th-floor psychiatric ward of the children's hospital. My son's father, me, my boyfriend and my best friend who is also Nick's care provider, all sat staring at each other as we waited for the first Child Family Team (CFT) meeting to being. The waiting room is deep inside the hospital in one of the towers that sits off from the main entrance quite a ways, so when the waiting room began to fill up with people, I was wondering if this was going to be like all the doctors' visits I've been to, you know, hurry up and wait for them to call someone else's name. A woman came out of the room that was now being blocked by standing waiters.

"Nicholas Raleigh CFT will take place in here." She announced. And the *entire waiting room* stood and began to file into the room. About a dozen people other than my team of four, took their seats. We all situated ourselves, some of us had pens and paper, some had notebooks and briefcases. We were all quiet, and waiting – I wasn't sure for who, but I knew we were waiting for the keystone. About thirty seconds went by and then the door cracked open. A tall skinny man in a white coat came in holding coffee with his glasses resting slightly on his forehead. "Is this for Nick?"

he asked. He came in and some of the people in the room stood for him. "Hello Doctor," the whole room mumbled and there he was, The Wizard of this Oz. He was the doctor.

For privacy purposes we will just call him, "Doctor" but he for some reason seemed to demand more respect instantly than any doctor I had seen in a while. "Hello, are you Mom?" He was very nice immediately, "Yes, hello I am Nick's Mom." He sipped his coffee and set it down, "Well, Helllllloooo Nick's Mom, I have been waiting to meet you, missy."

"And I am guessing this handsome man is his Dad y'all look like twins..." And he extended his hand to Nick's Dad. "Yes sir, good to meet you." We went around the room and everyone introduced themselves. Two Mercy Maricopa representatives, two liaisons from the hospital, Nick's new DDD case worker and a trainee, three agencies with BCBA Masters who was looking to evaluate Nick, someone from Arizona Healthcare Cost Containment Systems (AHCCCS), a high needs special case worker from a behavioral services center and his liaisons were there, and when we got back to the doctor, he introduced himself as the head doctor of psychiatry for the entire hospital and was pretty much the guy who made decisions, so he was on this case for many reasons, but mostly because it interested him.

Nicholas was having psychotic episodes that would last into some hours. He was capable of amazing strength and he was not responding to any "PRN" medications they had tried. PRN comes from the Latin term *pro re nata* which essentially means "as needed". Some medications actually increased his psychosis and the doctor was concerned that Nicholas was something he called an "Ultra metabolizer". This term meant that though Nick was being given medications that were supposed to sedate him and bring him out of psychosis, he was metabolizing them so fast and/ or, not at all, that the medications had no chance of working in a fight or flight environment. Nick was what this doctor called, "a one percent of one percent kind of child". Nick was the perfect storm of symptoms and he himself had no idea how we had gone this long without medical help, keeping Nick safely maintained. His entire staff was having difficulty maintaining Nicholas during his rages. We discussed the day Nicholas was admitted (six days earlier) as an example.

They had administered a drug called Haldol when we first got into the ER. Then half an hour later a shot of Risperidone, and a shot of Valium right after that. Nicholas threw grown men and women off him and was viciously fighting the staff as they then called in security, who tied him to the bed.

He was tied to the bed and unable to "move," so they backed off from him. As soon as the last security guard left the room, Nick's Dad and I sat in the room looking at each other, He looked over to Nick and said, "Buddy, this is serious," and immediately Nicholas sat up (his shoulders nearly dislocated) and he flung his whole body tipping the bed onto two feet then slamming back to the ground, then he flung to the other side and tipped it on the other two feet and it slammed back down. Almost in slow motion, and with all his might he flung back to the other side and took the hospital bed to the ground on its side. The guards who had literally just started walking away all turned around and got to the window just as Nick took the bed onto its side. He screamed like a banshee and a doctor, a nurse and five security guards all flew back into the room, flipped the bed back onto its back, and the doctor yelled "MOM AND DAD NEED TO LEAVE NOW!"

Nick's Dad and I jumped up and into the hall. They were all struggling to secure the bed, and the restraints. He was pulling the restraints so hard they weren't holding him, and he was able to get a hand, then a leg, then the other hand free. The staff had no protocol for anything like this and it was very apparent. After a good 20-minute battle to get his hands restrained properly, Nick laughed loudly then fell asleep.

The doctor explained this whole situation to the room of experts and observers, and the entire room fell cricket-chirping quiet. "Any suggestions on how we handle this?" He folded his hands and looked around.

"Anyone? Because I personally have been a doctor longer than this Mom has been alive and I am at a loss. This is not the environment to keep him in and this is not going well."

And he was right. The whole thing was not going well. He had been in the hospital for six days at this point and they were having to tie Nicholas to the bed and restrain him for almost a third of the day. He lost all his natural circadian rhythm and was sleeping in the middle of the day, or for a few hours in the morning. All the children on the floor were terrified of him and the doctor was also there to discuss the fact they were needing to move him to a two-room suite because one room was for restraints and the other room would be for him to play and stay in. The reason being was he was associating the bed with being tied up and he was falling asleep in the bathroom or on the floor – he was developing a fear of lying in a bed because he was being tied up there. They had no other way of preventing him from hurting himself and others.

In a hospital that had to have two children to one room, Nick was now occupying two rooms for just himself. The medications changed almost daily, and the doctor was trying everything in cocktails and combinations. After week four and five they were into medications 14 and 15. They were running out of medications, so in an attempt to try to trick me, they began to use the same medications under different names. I would research each one and explain to the nurses that was already a medication they tried, and each time I was met with: "But not this combination." I received a call that the hospital staff was unable to understand Nick's needs after the first week he was there. I was unable to be there 24/7 to help them, so I sent his care provider to the hospital to assist the staff.

The agency he worked for waited five weeks before they informed us that they weren't able to pay him when he was in the hospital with Nicholas, because the hospital was being paid to watch Nicholas. I wrote a grievance explaining the hospital did not know how to tend to Nicholas and was calling his care provider for tips and tricks, and when they still couldn't provide adequate care, I sent them adequate care. The state ignored me, and refused to pay him – but he still kept going, every single day.

Week eight came and so did the CFT meeting. Each one started out the same. "Anyone have any suggestions on what to do?" The doctor would ask, and the suggestions each week started to flat out get quite stupid, and silly. They went from wanting to release him into a boys' home, or to an expansion home (basically a smaller version of a placement home). But then when they provided that as a choice, you see, it never really was an option. No expansion home exists that can and will take Nicholas. No boys home exists that can and will take him. He was under the age of 12, non-verbal, and still needed diapers, he was not able to fit the criteria of any home they could find. By "they" I mean, noone – not a single agency in the state of Arizona could figure out what to do with Nick. The talks went on for hours, every single week, and every single week Nicholas sat in the hospital, nothing was done to perpetuate a release until one day.

During this particular week medications 21 and 22 had been tried (and were failing), and it marked the 10th week that Nick had occupied two rooms in the psychiatry ward. The entire time Nicholas was in that hospital my whole world was just barely functioning. I worked, I went home, I was at the hospital or on the phone asking questions, seeking answers.

The 10th week CFT meeting started like the first meeting except this time there were about 30 people in the room. The doctor was not at this meeting but his liaisons were. We had almost the same amount of people on a conference call as we did in the room, and the tension from the get-go was high. A lady on the phone began to discuss homes for Nicholas in Florida, North Carolina, and Ontario, Canada. She was using a lot of acronyms and she was being very nonchalant about the fact she was talking about sending a 10-year-old child to another state for placement. But even worse, she then said, "Well (speaking to someone in the room who was her counterpart) we can just vet options offline and get back to the group with their choices." I muted the phone and looked at the hospital liaison and asked, "Did she just say she is going to vet choices for me and then present me with the best choice she chose?" The liaison shook her head, "Yeah, that's what I just got from that too." I stopped the woman on the phone and looked to her counterpart, "Excuse me, ma'am whoever you are, if my son's name is on any documents or a part of any conversations it is my right as his parent to hear or see anything that is being VETTED for the placement and ongoing care of my child, DO YOU UNDER-STAND?"

She sat there for a second, she said, "I'm sorry we don't discuss company protocol and policy with clients." I stopped the entire meeting, "Ma'am, excuse me, per my rights as a parent, any docu-mentation penned or conversations held regarding my son for the ongoing care of him and the quality of his life will have me in them, and you will not skirt around that with company policy and protocol jargon – do you understand I am that Mom who reads your policy booklets. And per page 57, of your booklet, the parents or guardians will be a part of and have say so to any place-ment options being discussed for their child. Would you like me to pull it out and read it to you verbatim because I am paraphras-ing, but I believe it says nearly those exact words." She was silent, then she scoffed, "Well, I –" I interrupted her, "Well, you, just go ahead and CC me on any emails or conversations ya'll might be having, otherwise you will not be happy with the resulting com-plaint, thank you and we may move along now." The room was silent, and she quietly said, "Yes, I understand." The tension was more than most of us could take so I ended the meeting that day.

As I walked out of the cramped and very hot room, one person who had been at several of my meetings (they were all nameless faces at that point) came up to me and said, "You need to call this lady." And he walked off. Her name and number were written in pencil, and it said "Call her ASAP" at the bottom. I can't say who gave me that number but you know who you are, and if you are reading this – I wish you could understand the amount of grati-tude I have, thank you.

She stood about 5 feet 1 inch tall and was not who I expected. She was very tightlipped, had steel grey hair and wore gold-framed glasses. We were sitting in that same old familiar waiting room, waiting to go into Week 11's CFT. "Hello, are you Nick's mom?" I introduced myself and Nick's Dad, and his care provider. "Can we talk for a few minutes before the circus starts?" I had only spoken with her briefly on the phone once and I wasn't really sure what she did or who she was, but she was who I needed to speak with. It was day 81 and we were struggling to make heads or tails of what was even happening.

So, who was she? She was an attorney. Her specialty... special needs and disability cases. Nicholas was now not sleeping, he was bouncing off walls, breaking computers and tablets as they gave them to him; he was running wild at all hours, he was out of school for two months now, and they were cycling through medications like it was a food menu.

She sat with us quietly and observed. She said only her name during the introductions part and she wrote, the entire time.

The doctor walked in, greeted me and my family kindly, but sat down and immediately went ballistic at everyone else at the table. Particularly ballistic at the representative from the insurance company that was paying all the agencies that were sitting there twiddling their thumbs and who had now taken a backburner position in figuring anything out. "WHAT ARE YOU EVEN DOING HERE? YOU WRITE NOTES, YOU SAY YOU WILL TALK WITH YOUR BOSS AND WHO IS YOUR BOSS? IS HE ON VACATION??!!"

The representative was so upset that she excused herself and went running out of the room crying. The doctor looked at everyone, "There is a little boy who has been sitting in my hospital for almost three months, there is nothing SO WRONG with him that he should be in this environment any longer, get him the hell out of here and dammit I mean it, you all better stop messing around, this is unacceptable." He said very calmly, after screaming at the girl. The meeting ended and that day he was removed from our case. The hospital made him call and record his apology, and I told him to save it, that the fact he has to apologize is disgusting. He said to them exactly what he should have said and I appreciated him. He laughed and said, "Well thank you, your son is very lucky to have you as a Mom." And that was the last time he was allowed to be on our case, or to see my son; but what happened next was a miracle – at the next CFT meeting, we had an attorney representing us.

"You can be pitiful or powerful, you cannot be BOTH."

Joyce Myers

12 THE EXTREMELY F*CKED UP MEDICATION TRIAL PERIOD

"**H**ello, I am an attorney working with the family." Those words were like magic beans to Jack, like the glass slipper to Cinderella – they made everyone treat us differently, work with haste, develop clear ideas before speaking, and the unfavorable options that were being doled out as choices were all rescinded. When the attorney was there people acted as though they had some sense. The only person who had cared about getting a good result was taken off my case, but that was OK. My son's new doctor, the liaisons, caseworkers, and their trainees, all the behavioral people, began to formulate a plan to actually release my son. When placement began to clearly not be an actual option for Nick, I again asked "Why can't he be brought home?"

This was something that had been asked extensively. I asked, the doctor asked, everyone was asking and we were always met with a "Certain criteria" speech from the insurance reps and DDD. You see, as a parent no one ever told me I could speak up and ask questions, that is why throughout this entire book I am advocating and cheering you on to *please, yes – do ask questions* and this is the ultimate, stirring moment as to why:

We were entering the 12th week of Nicholas being in the hospital, and this marked a serious situation for two reasons. The first being at the three-month mark, Nicholas's residency was now considered "changed", and I had to formally call Social Security and change his address to the hospital. The second being that my son was hitting day 90 in the hospital, and no one knew *why.*

"What criteria are you referring to?" the attorney asked. For the first time in almost three months the DDD rep spoke up,

"Yes, there is a fifty-something page release order here and it outlines the amount of care Nicholas is required to have in order to get out of the hospital." "*A what?*" I almost yelled, as half the room gasped and began to mumble. There were about 25 of the 30 people in the "loop" of this case sitting in this tiny room and no one had ever mentioned this order for release, not one time!

"Yeah, blah blah it's a fifty-blah page document...blah blah blah blah.." *That's what I thought I heard.* "Who wrote it?" I asked. "I'm sorry, what did you say?" He looked like a deer caught in the headlights of a truck. "I am, uh, hold on," His boss was on the phone, and quickly interjected, "We have never been asked to produce that information, please give us some time to ascertain the origin of this report." I looked at the attorney, puzzled, as I continued, "What do you mean you have never been asked that? Does that mean you don't know who wrote it?" I looked at the guy sitting there shuffling through papers, and the phone went quiet. I sat quietly and waited for an answer.

"Well, no," one of the directors the special needs division of DDD said on the conference call finally answered. The attorney asked "Wait, you don't know who wrote the criteria of release for this patient?" and the line once again was very quiet. "I'm sorry – who is speaking to me?" the DDD Director asked. "I am an attorney working with the family," our attorney explained. The DDD Directors candor became very robotic, "I cannot continue this conversation we must seek legal representation. I am instructing the caseworker and all DDD personnel to please leave this meeting immediately and contact me when you have. Thank you, I am sorry but I cannot continue to speak on this agency's behalf, we must terminate our meeting without legal representation present." Click. Both the caseworker and trainee for DDD who were in the room stood up and left, and we decided to end the meeting that day.

It took them three days to get back to me and tell me who wrote the release. It only took the attorney working with us a couple hours. She called her connections and found out that not only was it two different doctors, both had never actually laid eyes on Nick and they were using the notes from the hospital's nurses.

We had another CFT that week and this time it was just the main people involved with Nicholas. We all sat and went down the release order and started figuring out exactly what bringing him home would look like, who would cover the hours. We also revised a lot of the third-hand knowledge and had someone who was in a position to observe him first hand go in and work with the doctor who was writing this release order, and help them better understand the ongoing needs of Nicholas and also his family team.

I mentioned that his care provider was not being paid for the weeks and weeks he had been in the hospital. The entire table of people agreed that this was unacceptable and the hospital would either need to cough up that money or the hours would need to be approved. By the grace of God, they approved his care provider's hours for the almost 13 weeks he was with Nick in the hospital without pay.

The people in the right places were finally listening, placing him at home with in-home services was the only way to get him stable, but we needed intense behavioral services or it was never going to work. We needed a place that could provide services, and a psychiatrist who could work closely with the team to ensure the longevity of success for Nick's outpatient care. We found that in a place called Touchstone. They were the only ones who were willing to take this situation head on, use the program they had in place, and accommodate the situation for what it was.

After a long arduous process of designing what bringing him home would look like, 103 days after checking him in, Nicholas was released from the hospital and brought home with wrap-around 24/7 services, and a huge list of medications.

I asked for a print-out of his medical records, and the document was so big it was printed on both sides and still extended to over 1000 pages! The notes, exams, observations, lists and lists of medications and incident reports of Nick injuring someone. I couldn't believe the number and amount of medications and different attending doctors he had. It was like a revolving door of medications. They called me to ask me if they could tweak his meds, and they called me often to do this. Little was I aware they were just adding more and more to the already fleeting few that had some effect.

When he was released from the hospital Nicholas was on nine medications. the list was as follows;

- Perphenazine (Antipsychotic medication)
- Hydroxyzine (Anti-anxiety medication)
- Seroquel XR (Antipsychotic medication)
- Propranolol (Hypertension, Anti-anxiety medication)
- Risperidone (Antipsychotic medication)
- Oxycodone (Pain medication)
- Ibuprofen 800 (Anti-inflammatory medication)
- Prozac (Antidepressant)
- Buspirone (Anti-anxiety medication)

I am not a doctor. I have taken some physiology and anatomy courses. I was a sports athletic trainer in high school, and at one time I was pre-med in college, but I was not, and am not, a medical professional. With that said, when I read the release medications list, my jaw dropped. My ten-year-old son was taking enough medication to tranquilize a linebacker. He was on pain medications? I never actually agreed to those, and still to this day have no idea why Nicholas was put on pain medications. They said he "appeared to be in pain" at times and while I thought they would give him Tylenol, they gave him Percocet.

When they called to tell me he appeared to be angry all the time, they wanted to give him a combination of medications at therapeutic doses so that he could sleep. They were giving him medications that weren't for sleep, they gave him medications to slow his heart rate, and anti-anxiety medications. I thumbed through the nearly 1000-page medical stay report, and began a list of medications in a quadrant. I split a piece of printer paper into four squares and labeled each square accordingly: Anti-anxiety medications, Antipsychotic medications, Antidepressant medications, and other. I looked up each medication and began to sort them all into the aforementioned categories. The list was so vast and as I suspected their cycling through medications under different names was a common practice, and where one would call Buspirone just that, the next would call it Buspar and retry the medication again in combination with something else or in a different dosage. Below is the final list I had before me when I had finished listing and researching each medication

Nicholas was prescribed the following list of medications in a 103-day period:

- **Anti-Anxiety Medications**
- Alprazolam (Xanax)
- Lorazepam (Ativan)
- Buspirone (BusPar)
- Escitalopram (Lexapro)
- Hydroxyzine
- Diazepam (Valium)
- Gabapentin
- Duloxetine (Cymbalta)

- Paroxetine (Paxil)
- Clonidine
- Propranolol
- Venlafaxine (Effexor XR)
- Clonazepam (Klonopin)
- Stadol (Injection)
- **Antipsychotic Medications**
- Aripiprazole (Abilify)
- Risperidone (Risperdal, M tab)
- Ziprasidone (Geodon)
- Olanzapine (Zyprexa)
- Perphenazine (Trilafon)
- Haldol (oral and injection)
- Divalproex (Depakote)
- Thorazine
- Quetiapine (Seroquel)
- **Antidepressants**
- Celexa
- Wellbutrin
- Fluoxetine (Prozac)
- Zoloft
- **Other Medications**
- Oxycodone (Percocet)
- Ibuprofen 800

Each medication was used in cocktails with others. Nothing about how it affected his behavior or sleep was tracked or documented, for each cocktail, so when he was released with all these medications with very little data or justifications, I immediately went to his team and the ongoing attending psychiatrist. I told them right up front I was not comfortable with the medications they released him with. Some of them were serious mind-altering medications that we would need to take into consideration and discuss what each one was prescribed for, and we would need to discuss why each one would need to continue. I presented my case for removing all the antipsychotics. Not all at once, but one at a time because Nicholas is not psychotic and most of the antipsychotic medications had very bad side effects that Nicholas could not describe, or tell us he was experiencing.

One-by-one we phased out all the medications that made me feel uncomfortable for Nick. Some were hell to be phased out. Seroquel was one of them. As we began to back off certain medications we began to notice that Nicholas was anxious so I would research all the medications in that category and look at his medical record and look at the notes following each time they administered a medication, and on my own whim and research, working very carefully with a doctor who listened to me and knew I was not some layman that didn't know my son, we slowly weaned Nicholas down to four medications that are now given in very low doses.

Coupled with very intensive services, having the team learn BCBA techniques and having an intensive behavioral training program headed by a trained expert has saved our whole lives.

After "playing with" Nick's medications, then adding supplements to his daily medication regimen to ensure he has a well-balanced vitamin intake, he started declining in self-injurious and aggressive behaviors. I modified my home as much as I could, and I learned that things are only things – they break, they get torn and broken. I had to accept that. And if we are being truly honest, as a parent I had to change a lot. I was allowing only half-assed efforts from everyone even myself, and when a very candid care provider sat me down and gave me a "Come to Jesus" talk, I knew it was with my decisions and actions that this whole situation would live and die.

My effort to conform to what Nick needed was the last thing that needed to fall in to place. I pressured everyone to also conform and "drink-the-Kool-Aid" and as we got up each day and went back at it, stayed consistent and made sure we were all on the same page; days that were barely sustainable, became not so bad. And each day as it passes, seems to get better and better.

The program that came into our lives that made the most difference was a very small unit in a behavioral therapy program called "Whatever it Takes," at the time we came home from hospital this was a 90-day in and out program that was designed to meet the child where they were, and get them to where they needed to be, in a small amount of time. Once we got home it became clear this was not going to be a short-term thing, and so the behavioral therapy company we went through used our intense (two providers in my home 24-hours-a-day) in-home program to pilot a quicker, more responsive and comprehensive program to help severe mental issues and crisis situations for younger children than had previously been accounted for.

The company and its constituents study the integrity of our data to understand the efficacy of this very hands-on ABA skill acquisition plan that came to the rescue and provided a bridge for the gap in services that was astoundingly evident, yet were not being remedied otherwise. If it were not for several people in this company working in collaboration around the clock, our lives could have turned out very differently. It was with great hope we all went into this process, and, so far, we have challenged whole systems, created new policy, changed old policies, and paved the way for children like Nick to get the help they truly need.

"If you own this story, you get to write the ending."

Brene Brown

13 CONCLUDING WORDS OF ENCOURAGEMENT

So, this first part may not seem encouraging, but bear with me. After six months Nicholas was beginning to really adapt to the whole new program at home. I finally started to see the results of our team effort, and then one day, out of the blue, a devastating tragedy took place that was almost the straw that made the camel's back buckle.

On October 29, 2017, Nick's Dad was at his friend's house for a Halloween party, when he saw his friend's neighbors fighting. Being the hero he always was, he went to break it up and was stabbed and killed immediately. There was nothing anyone could have done, he died almost instantly.

Nick's father and I had a very tumultuous past; in some ways I felt like he was a permanent fixture. He was just there, always – no matter if I wanted him there or not – and when it wasn't an option for him to be there anymore, the reality set in that I was in this life situation with Nick alone again. For real this time. He wasn't just not here in the now, he was gone, in the forever sense. Some days I imagine him to be off somewhere I can still get to, and then there are days that feel like him being gone couldn't be any more soul crushing than it has been. Nicholas is non-verbal and when his Dad was killed in such a quick "here today, gone tomorrow" fashion it was very tough for him to register the magnitude of that loss.

He sometimes *still* piles stuff by the door, hunts down a picture of his Dad and requests him. Yeah, my heart isn't just broken, it's simply like dust some days. But then there are days that Nicholas writes his name, has no bad behaviors – he dances with me, hikes with me and wraps his arms around me to show me he loves me; and my heart is so full and big it almost explodes, and I begin to wonder if his Dad is helping me from the other side.

In the beginning, I said that this was my struggle, my journey, and being Nicholas's Mom now defines me as a human being; but this isn't about just me – this is about "we".

This is *our* struggle and *our* journey, and as a parent, I guess I am doing this alone, but I am not alone. I have a community of care providers, and true friends cheering us on. My parents and some of my family do what they can to provide moral support, but as far as being included in Nick's daily routines and daily life, they take a backseat, and that's okay, this isn't a situation everyone can handle. I never thought I could end up here, actually handling it. This is a lifelong challenge but I can finally face it with hope, not fear; love and understanding, not anger and pain.

In thirteen years on this earth, Nicholas has never said, "I love you Mom," but I know he loves me. It's in the way he looks at me and smiles, kisses me as he walks by me, and cheerfully pulls me to his room and shuts the door in glee as he sits me down and pats my head. Nicholas is the last piece I have of his Dad, and he has taught me about what being kind and patient really means. If you never give up, and never give in, the world can never crush you; if you always remember to just breathe and remind yourself, this too shall pass. I hope you are better for having read this in one way or another, may my words find you well, but in the event that you are sitting there wondering if you are crazy, or if there might be something wrong with your child, may this book give you a guide as to what to do and not do. I wish you and your loved ones the best, good luck! And God Speed, my friend.

Thank you!

To everyone who has every worked with Nicholas and has gotten us to today. No words can convey my gratitude and appreciation, even though some of you probably think I am a "mom"ster, I hope you can understand, I am fierce, and always have been, for Nick.

BEST REGARDS,
NICK'S MOM

Printed in the USA
CPSIA information can be obtained
at www.ICGtesting.com
LVHW061031141223
766499LV00017B/33